BYRON - THE HUNTSMAN

- US MARSHAL

By

JAMES GARDINER

Copyright © [2024] by James Gardiner]

All rights reserved.

No portion of this book may be reproduced in any form without written permission from the publisher or author except as permitted by U. S. Copyright law.

JAMES GARDINER

BYRON - THE HUNTSMAN - US MARSHAL

CONTENTS

Foreword 1
Introduction 2
Byron, The Huntsman, Us Marshal 4
A Man Who Killed, Because He Loved Killing 33
Jackson Hole Badlands 49
Not Planned To Join A Raid With Outlaws 61
He Was Terrified Just Like The Rest 75
Too Many Dead Bodies 90
Heavily Armed And Well-Trained Men 104
The Necessity For An Anaesthetic 117
The Van De Velt House 145
A Journey To Abigail's House 164
His Skinning Knife Finding Its Mark 178
Abigail Emerged Onto The Porch 198
Forced Him Into Uncharacteristic Situations 214
Pursuing Van De Velt 222
Montana, The Final Frontier 230
Recognition Dawned 253
The Vendetta Weighed Heavily On Him 273
Byron Arrived At The Rio Grande 287
Daniel Van De Velt 308
Blurbs 323
About The Author 324

FOREWORD

In the vast urban landscapes of America, U.S. Marshal Byron, "The Huntsman," was a symbol of justice. His unyielding pursuit of criminals earned him legendary status. Yet, a personal loss transformed his mission into a dark crusade for revenge. This foreword invites you to witness Byron's journey from law enforcer to avenger as he delves into the criminal underworld, challenging the very essence of justice.

INTRODUCTION

Byron: The Huntsman's Vengeance unfolds in the heart of America's urban jungle, where Byron, a U. S. Marshal known as "The Huntsman," is revered as a symbol of justice. His relentless pursuit of felons has made him a legend.

However, when personal tragedy strikes, it ignites a thirst for vengeance, leading him down a perilous path. As Byron infiltrates a ruthless gang, he faces the ultimate test: maintaining his moral compass in a world where he is both the predator and the prey.

This gripping narrative delves into the complexities of justice, the psychology of revenge, and the sacrifices one must make.

I want to express my deepest gratitude to my wife, whose unwavering support and belief in my work have been my anchor through the years. Her patience and love have been the quiet force behind this journey.

To her, I dedicate not only this book but all my endeavours.

1

BYRON, THE HUNTSMAN, US MARSHAL

As twilight descended, he materialised at the outskirts of the town, a sudden and unsettling presence. His arrival was not direct; he paused just beyond the initial buildings, perched on his imposing stallion. There, he studied the street ahead with an eerie stillness. After a brief moment, seemingly satisfied, he urged his horse forward, moving down the main street. A formidable figure clad in a weathered coat, he became an enigma woven into the growing darkness.

Beyond the initial impression of a typical cowboy, subtle nuances distinguished him from the crowd. His attire, though rugged, bore an unexpected tidiness unlike the typical grime associated with wandering cowboys. His duster coat—popularised by the use of the Union Cavalry, a light, loose, and long coat made of canvas fitted with a slit up the back for easy riding—was worn to protect riders' clothing from dirt. Still, the road dust clung to him less fervently, hinting at a life beyond the open prairies. Perhaps he was more than a mere rider; possibly, he carried secrets woven into the fabric of his coat. Moreover, his gaze held a certain intensity, an awareness that transcended the mundane. It lingered on the town's architecture, the people bustling about, and the hidden corners where shadows whispered their secrets.

His eyes, framed by the battered hat, betrayed a curiosity beyond the thrill of the ride. They were windows into a world unseen, a realm where asphalt met enigma. As he eased his steed forward, the pace softened, almost as if it recognised the uniqueness of its rider. The townsfolk glanced, some with suspicion, others with intrigue. This man was not merely passing through; he carried stories etched into the leather saddlebags, carved into the lines on his weathered face. And so, as dusk settled, he became more than a silhouette against the fading light.

He became a question mark, an enigma wrapped in mystery. This mystery lingered long after he disappeared around the bend. The weather went unnoticed by most, but some details set this rider apart: a fusion of menace and mystery. From the top of his duster coat protruded the handle of a pistol, a silent sentinel. But more intriguing was the heavy-calibre rifle, its elongated barrel in a saddle scabbard beneath his left leg. Within easy reach, it awaited its purpose. But his eyes, the windows to a hidden narrative, betrayed him. Hard and black, they glittered with a cold intensity above a heavy black veil. These were not the eyes of a mere traveller; they held secrets etched in shadows, whispered across desolate landscapes. Perhaps he rode not for leisure but for purpose, an enigma wrapped in his coat, a riddle veiled by the steps of his steed.

Certainly, though maybe a wanderer of trails, the stranger did not fit the mould of a cowhand earning a daily wage. His purpose remained veiled, a mystery woven into the fabric of his existence. As he continued down the street, his gaze remained fixed ahead, yet it roved incessantly, missing nothing on either side. This was no ordinary journey; it was an exploration, an unravelling of secrets hidden within the town's narrow confines.

The town was a mere whisper in the landscape, a minimal existence clinging to its one main street. Short, sharp streets crisscrossed like the etchings of forgotten memories. These were not grand boulevards but intimate alleyways, each bearing its tale. No more than a couple of dozen buildings stood as silent witnesses. He imagined their walls harbouring stories untold. And so, the stranger moved, a sentinel of enigma, through the heart of this quiet town. His eyes, ever watchful, held the weight of unspoken histories. Perhaps he sought answers or carried them, etched into the lines on his weathered face. The horse's steps echoed through the narrow passages, a refrain that whispered: Here, in the shadows, lies the truth.

In this quaint little town, where Main Street winds its way through the heart of simplicity, the hotel is a silent witness to the past and the flow of life. Its weathered facade, adorned with faded signs and creaking shutters, tells tales of countless travellers who sought refuge within its walls. The cowboy, clad in a duster coat, halted the magnificent stallion. His eyes, ever alert, held the burden of unspoken histories. Perhaps he sought answers or carried them, carved into the lines on his weathered face. The horse's steps echoed through the narrow passages.

One thing that made him stand out was his horse. It was not a common breed but a rare and magnificent specimen. Its coat was a glossy black, shining in the dim light. Its mane and tail were long and silky, flowing with every movement. Its muscles were well-defined, showing its strength and agility. Its eyes were dark and intelligent, matching its rider's. It was a horse of noble blood, a descendant of the finest Arabian horses. It was a horse that could endure long journeys, cross harsh terrains, and outrun any pursuer. It was a horse that commanded respect and admiration. It was a horse that matched its rider, a companion of mystery.

The stranger had acquired the horse in a distant land, where he had encountered many adventures and dangers. The horse had saved his life more than once, and he had saved the horse's. They had formed a bond of trust and loyalty, a friendship transcending words. They had travelled many miles together, seen many sights, and shared many secrets. They were a pair of enigmas, a duo of mystery. The horse was more than a means of transportation; it was a part of his identity, a reflection of his soul.

The horse's steps subsided, leaving a quiet stretching across the cobblestones behind. His eyes scanned the surroundings: the worn-out awning, the flickering neon sign, and the promise of respite.

Deliberation hung in the air like a suspended breath. Perhaps memories tugged at him: the open road, the wind in his hair, the distant horizon. Or it could be the allure of the unknown, the anticipation of what lay beyond the next bend. And then, with a decisive motion, he swung his leg over the saddle. The ground met his boots, and the horse settled into stillness.

The cowboy stood there, a solitary figure against the saloon's "Catrine House" backdrop. His gaze lingered as if imprinting the scene upon his soul.

Quickly, he stepped towards the entrance. The door creaked open, revealing a dimly lit interior, a haven of mismatched furniture, and the scent of old wood. The big stallion rested, its black, well-groomed hair gleaming in the fading light. It, too, had found its place in this unassuming town.

And so, the saloon held its secrets, the stories etched into its walls, the whispered conversations, the fleeting encounters. Each guest left a mark, a fragment of their journey. The weight of miles and memories eased with every breath. In this small town, where time moved at its own pace, the bar stood as a refuge for wanderers, a chapter in their tales. And the stranger? He was just another chapter, turning the page and seeking solace in the embrace of four walls.

The main street outside continued its rhythm, the hum of life, and the passing moments. And the saloon, with its flickering sign, remained a silent witness.

His hands, bound to the hilt of the hefty rifle, tugged at the borrowed path out of its sheath. Yet wisdom, or instinct, prevailed, and he firmly repositioned the rifle, concealing it once more beneath the thick blanket. The window beckoned—a portal to the outside world. His gaze swept the view, assessing the risks. The glass doors stood sentinel, shielding most of his body from prying eyes. A fleeting glance inside the dimly lit bar, the patrons huddled over their secrets, offered a semblance of reassurance.

With purpose, he stepped across the threshold. The air shifted as if acknowledging his presence. To his left, the war-scarred wall bore witness to countless tales of laughter, whispered confessions, and glasses clinking. The table, its surface etched with memories, held court for weary travellers and rugged souls. And then, their eyes met—the strangers, a tribe unto themselves. Weathered faces, inked skin, stories etched in every line. Recognition flickered—a nod, a silent camaraderie.

Boulder, the grizzled veteran, a legend in these parts, held his gaze. The newcomer, an enigma, veiled his intentions. The bar beckoned—a sanctuary of liquid courage and unspoken truths. He approached, boots scuffing the worn floor. The bartender, a keeper of secrets, wiped a glass with practised ease. No questions asked, just a tilt of the head.

The newcomer leaned in, voice low, and ordered his poison—a shot of redemption, perhaps. The room absorbed his presence, but his eyes, the windows to a hidden story, exposed him. Hard and black, they sparkled with a cold intensity above a heavy black veil. These were not the eyes of a mere traveller; they held secrets carved in shadows, whispered across desolate landscapes. Perhaps he rode not for pleasure but for a reason, a mystery wrapped in his coat, a puzzle concealed by the steps of his steed. Surely, though perhaps a wanderer of trails, the stranger did not match the mould of a cowhand earning a daily wage. His motive remained hidden, a mystery woven into the very fabric of his being.

Unspoken truths lingered in the creaking floorboards, the flickering bulbs, and the weight of unspoken stories. The cowboy's journey had led him here to this crossroads of fate. The rifle, now concealed, whispered promises of protection and peril. The past clung to him—the open plains, the battles fought, the scars both seen and hidden. And so, he stood alone, wandering in a room full of echoes. The bar was a sanctuary for lost souls, cradling his secrets. The glass doors framed his exit, but destiny lingered. The hustle and bustle of life outside raged on, but within these walls, time stood still.

The cowboy's footsteps echoed, merging with the pulse of the bar. His purpose remained veiled, and his story remained untold. The room, with its worn tables and flickering bulbs, held its breath. The dimly lit bar held its secrets, woven into the grain of the ancient wood.

A weathered soul, the bartender moved with practised ease in a dance between glass and liquid. The shadows whispered Bobby's name. He navigated the hallowed space, fetching more drinks, a ritual of solace for the weary. And then, like a ghost emerging from the mist, Bobby returned. In his hands, a big mug of beer, foam trailing down one side, was a promise of warmth and oblivion. Half a bottle of whisky, its amber depths calling to those who sought refuge. The glass, chipped but usable, contained tales of countless toasts.

The stranger, perched on a stool, leaned into the bar. His hands, rough-hewn, rested on the sacred surface.

"Oh yeah, yeah, sure," he murmured, as if acknowledging some unspoken truth.

His attention shifted to the whisky, which danced slowly on his lips. Sip by deliberate sip, he savoured the burn, memories surfacing like forgotten dreams. Half-slouched, defying gravity, his feet, planted beneath him, held the tension of a coiled spring. The room buzzed with anticipation, as if the air held its breath. The stranger's eyes sharpened, assessing the room. He was no mere traveller; he was a sentinel, attuned to every heartbeat.

In the corner, a silent exchange unfolded. One of the men at the rear table, with a scar across his cheek and eyes like flint, nodded to another. A nudge, a shared understanding. The second man, grinning like a naughty child, rose from his chair. His steps were deliberate; he was a measured predator, closing in on prey. No questions hung in the air. No whispered conspiracies. Just purpose.

The stranger, unyielding, took no notice of his thoughts. His gaze remained fixed on the bar and Bobby's weathered face. The room held its breath, a tableau frozen in time. And then, as if surrendering to destiny, the second man reached the bar. Their eyes met in a silent negotiation. Hidden from prying eyes, what transpired next would ripple through the room. The whisky, the beer, and the chipped glass all bore witness. The stranger's fingers twitched, ready for action.

The stranger's presence shifted the balance in this dim sanctuary, where secrets mingled with smoke. And Bobby, the storekeeper, poured another drink, his eyes reflecting the dance of fate. The other man, a shadow in the dim-lit room, approached the swinging doors. His movements were precise, fingers tracing invisible patterns on the wood until the hinges groaned under the weight. And then, with purpose, he stepped through the threshold, his gaze piercing the darkness.

The stranger, seated at the bar, felt the weight of scrutiny. In a silent exchange, his eyes met the man's challenge. As a witness, his horse stood outside. Secrets were hidden within its heart. And then the man spoke in a voice that cut through the bare murmur.

"Now, where did someone like you get a horse like that?" he exclaimed, as if unravelling a mystery.

The room held its breath, and the air was thick with anticipation. In the inky-black night, what lay beyond the glass? Only the stranger knew the road, the horizon, and the next chapter of his journey. The stranger's gaze trailed the man's in this twilight realm, where fate hung precariously. The swinging doors swung shut, sealing their unspoken pact. The air in the bar thickened with tension woven from whisky fumes and unspoken challenges.

The stranger, a cipher in his coat, sat at the scarred bar, his gaze unwavering. The man by the door, Finley, a mountain of muscle and scars, had thrown down the gauntlet. His broken nose, a testament to the battles fought, flared as he squared off.

"You're not?" the manager's voice cut through the haze, eyes narrowing.

The stranger remained still, like a sentinel in dim light. His fingers traced the rim of the whisky glass, seeking solace or resolve. Safety, perhaps, lay in the amber depths.

"Hey," the man by the door said, eyes gleaming with mischief. "I am asking you a question."

The stranger's silence was a challenge, a dare. And then the man by the door, who would nudge fate, stepped forward. Finley, aptly named, loomed like a storm cloud. His massive head, crowned with a broken nose, held stories etched in bone. His eyes, the colour of bruised plums, narrowed as he assessed the stranger.

"Is that your stallion?" Finley repeated, his voice a blade.

The stranger's gaze swept Finley, sizing him up. A sip of whisky burned as a counterpoint to the room's tension. And then, defiance, raw and unyielding, spilt forth.

"Where I come from," the stranger drawled, "it's kind of unhealthy to take a whole lot of interest in another man's horse."

His words hung in the air, a challenge flung across the bar. A standoff of wills linked them. Surprised, Finley hesitated. Fear was a foreign language to him, yet this stranger spoke it fluently. For a moment, indecision flickered in his eyes. Back off or press forward? The men at the table watched, anticipation etched on their faces. To bite down now would be to lose face-to-face; no one dared risk it.

The stranger's defiance echoed in this smoky arena, where honour and ego clashed. The stallion outside stood as a symbol of freedom and recklessness. Unspoken challenges. The stranger sat at the scarred bar, his gaze unwavering. Finley, the man by the door, had confronted the challenge. As he squared off, his broken nose flared, a testament to the battles fought. He shattered the bar's silence.

"Look," he said, as if revealing a secret.

Everyone in the bar held their breath, waiting for what he would say next. What was out there at night? Only he knew the road, the horizon, the next adventure. He locked eyes with the stranger in this twilight zone, where anything could happen. The doors swung closed, sealing their pact. The atmosphere in the bar grew tense—a mix of whisky and challenge.

The mystery stranger sat at the worn-out bar, his stare steady. The man by the door, Finley, a giant of muscle and scars, had issued the challenge. His crooked nose, a sign of fights won and lost, twitched as he faced him.

"You're not?" the manager's voice sliced through the fog, suspicious.

The stranger stayed calm, like a guard in the dim light. His fingers traced the edge of the whisky glass. The stranger's silence was a provocation, a risk. And then the man next door, who would change everything, moved forward. Finley, who was well-named, towered like a storm. His massive head was topped with a broken nose, carving stories into the bone. His eyes, the colour of old bruises, narrowed as he sized up the stranger.

"Is that your horse?" Finley repeated, his voice sharp.

The stranger's gaze scanned Finley, measuring him. A sip of whisky stung in contrast to the room's pressure. And then, defiance, pure and stubborn, poured out.

"Where I come from," the stranger drawled, "it's not very smart to be too curious about another man's horse."

His words lingered in the air, a challenge thrown across the bar. They stood together in a clash of wills. Finley hesitated, surprised. Fear was a language he didn't speak, but this stranger was fluent in. For a moment, doubt flickered in his eyes.

Back off or push on? The men at the table watched, eager to see what would happen. Backing down now would mean losing respect for fate; no one wanted to be tempted. The stranger's defiance echoed in this smoky place, where pride and ego collided. As a symbol of freedom and recklessness, the horse waited outside.

Finley decided to push on, unwilling to let the stranger get away with his attitude. He clenched his fists and took a step closer.

"You think you're tough, huh? Let's see how tough you are."

It all happened so fast that no one could figure out the exact sequence of events. The stranger leaned on the bar one second, casually drinking his whisky, while Finley approached him menacingly. The next second, Finley was lying on the floor, stunned and bleeding. The nearest bartender swore that the stranger had thrown his whisky in Finley's face, blinding him temporarily. He then swiftly placed his foot behind Finley's heel. The stranger then slammed his hand into Finley's nose, knocking him down with a single blow.

Finley bounced off the floor like a rubber ball, but the stranger didn't even spare him a glance. He calmly returned to the bar, poured another shot of whisky, and took a sip. He acted as if Finley was a minor annoyance, not a man who had just tried to attack him.

Finley staggered to his feet, his face red with anger and blood.

"You'll pay for this, you bastard!" he yelled.

He charged at the stranger, hoping to catch him off guard. But the stranger was ready. He put down his glass and dodged Finley's right hook, then landed a left jab on Finley's jaw. Finley grunted and leaned forward, stunned but not defeated. The stranger seized the opportunity, grabbed him by the hair, and pulled his head down with a violent jerk. The stranger smashed Finley's mouth against the edge of the bar with brutal force. The sound of flesh hitting wood and teeth shattering echoed in the room.

The stranger repeated his earlier move, hooking his foot behind Finley's heel and sending him tumbling to the floor. He casually picked up his drink and sipped it as if he had just swatted a fly, not a man. Finley lay on the floor for a while, his arms spread out. He slowly sat up, shaking his head and spitting out bits of teeth. He wiped his mouth with his hand and saw blood on it. He glared at his hand for a second and then let out a furious scream. He leapt to his feet and charged at the stranger again.

The stranger sighed, put down his drink, and dodged Finley's clumsy charge. He hit him in the back of the neck as he passed by, sending Finley crashing into the wall near the bar. He spun him around and punched Finley in the jaw with his left fist, stunning him momentarily. He then pushed his left palm against Finley's nose, tilting his head back and relaxing his stomach muscles. The stranger then delivered a hard, brutal punch to Finley's diaphragm. Air burst out of Finley's broken mouth, along with more blood and teeth. He folded over, gasping for air with a raspy sound.

What enraged Finley was the stranger's indifference. Every time he knocked Finley down, he would return to his drink as if bored with the fight. Finley struggled to breathe, and the stranger could have finished him off. He could have hit him harder, kicked him, or broken his bones. But he didn't. He treated him like a pesky mutt that could be scared away with a few rocks.

Finley couldn't stand the stranger's contempt. He knew that the men at his former table were laughing at him. They had never liked him because he liked to bully smaller men with his brute strength.

"You son of a bitch!" he snarled as he finally caught his breath.

He had a pistol on his right hip, and he reached for it as he crouched. He wanted nothing more than to kill the man who had humiliated him. The stranger was still leaning on the bar, sipping his whisky as if nothing had happened. The onlookers had been impressed by the stranger's skills, but now they were about to be astonished.

The stranger moved with incredible speed. One second, he held his whisky glass in his right hand. The next, he swapped it for his big Remington .44. Everyone dove, expecting a gunshot. Finley's pistol was still rising, but the stranger had already drawn his. But he didn't shoot. The stranger bashed the barrel of his pistol against Finley's wrist—hard, very hard. Finley howled in pain and dropped his gun.

The stranger, showing his first sign of anger, stepped forward and smashed his gun butt twice across Finley's face—right, then left. Finley staggered back, blood gushing from deep cuts. He would have fallen, but the stranger grabbed him by the front of his shirt, spun him around, and kicked him out of the bar doors, planting his boot deep into Finley's broad buttocks.

Finley flew out, shattering the glass as he went. He was vanishing into the night. The sound of his crash and thud echoed in the room as he hit the ground and rolled into the street. The stranger spun around to face the room, his .44 still in his grip. No one dared to move. The bartender was petrified, one hand hidden under the bar. He was wiping his brow nervously. He slowly lifted his hand, showing a dirty cloth he was holding. The men at the table where Finley had been sitting were silent, all hands visible on the table.

The stranger stared at them momentarily, alert, ready to act. Then, when it seemed they would stay still, he finally holstered his pistol, returned to the bar, and picked up his drink again. The bar was silent for another few minutes, except for a low murmur of conversation at the back table. Then, one of the men got up and started walking towards the stranger. It was the man who had first spoken—the man who had pushed Finley towards the stranger. He was a big man too, but of a completely different kind than Finley. He had more muscle than flab. He walked with confidence and balance. Every movement he made suggested speed. His face showed particular savage cruelty. But there was also something else: a code, a cunning threat lacking in Finley's furious rant.

Suddenly, the stranger was no longer leaning on the bar but standing upright, hands-free, with the whisky glass back on the bar. The big man approached him. They were both big men. The stranger towered over the other man, who was bulkier but shorter.

"Relax," the other man said. "Finley was a bastard. He had it coming."

The stranger spoke in a low voice. "I had a feeling you sent him to me."

The other man looked surprised. "Yeah, maybe. Maybe I did. I wanted to test your mettle. Did I pass?"

"Oh, yeah. Sure."

The other man grinned. "You're good; I'll give you that. You know how to fight. I respect that. I respect a man who can fend for himself. Here, let me get you a drink."

He gestured to the bartender, who poured two glasses of whisky. The stranger didn't move; his eyes were cold and hard.

"Aw, come on," the other man said. "Don't be sore. No hard feelings, right? We were having some fun. This place is dull as dirt. You spiced things up a bit. Come on, take the drink."

The man gestured to the bartender, who hurried over with another glass and filled both the stranger's and the man's glasses. The stranger finally nodded and reached for his glass. The other man flashed a crooked smile that revealed a missing tooth, picked up his glass, and raised it to his lips.

"Ross," he said. "People around here call me Boulder."

Byron raised his glass and nodded. "Just Byron, yeah."

He took a sip and grimaced. Boulder unconsciously flexed his massive shoulders and said, "Strange name, Boulder."

"Not really," Byron replied.

Suddenly, a loud clumping of boots echoed on the boardwalk outside. The saloon doors flew open with a bang. Finley appeared in the doorway, blood gushing from a deep gash on his forehead, his eyes wild with rage and pain, and with an enormous shotgun held in both hands.

"You bastard!" Finley screamed at Byron. "I'll blow you to hell!"

Byron owed his life to the shotgun's long barrel. The long barrel slowed down its aim, and when it finally pinpointed Byron's location, he had already moved, dodging to the right and Ross to the left. The shotgun's thunderous blast sent a shockwave so powerful that it caused the windows to swell outwards, and the massive spray of pellets flew past Byron by more than a foot, smashing a whole line of bottles on the bar.

Finley attempted to spin around to aim the shotgun at Byron again but was out of time. Byron had already drawn his gun and cocked it.

"Stick 'em up, fool!" he shouted, and an instant later, two hundred and fifty grains of lead tore through Finley's chest, splattering blood and flesh. Finley staggered backwards with a groan. The shotgun went off again in his hands, sending another blast of pellets into the air. Byron shot again, hitting Finley in the throat. Finley whirled around, crashed into the wall, and clawed desperately at his bleeding neck, then slowly slid down, leaving a broad streak of blood behind him. He lay dead against the wall.

The stranger whirled around to face the room. He relaxed after a moment. Off to the side, Ross stood with both hands in plain sight, far from the butt of his revolver. The remaining men at the rear table had dived for cover after the first blast of Finley's shotgun. They were too terrified to make another move. Byron slowly ejected the two empty shells from his pistol. He replaced them with fresh rounds and slipped the big Remington back into his holster.

Ross gave a small smile. "You have a good shot with a pistol. Perhaps even better than using your hands. How good are you at other things?"

"Do you want to find out?"

Ross shook his head. "No, I've had enough excitement for tonight."

He turned to the bar, where their glasses were still present. He grabbed his, then gave the other one to Byron.

"Cheers," he said, still smiling.

Byron, with a blank face, lifted his glass and drank. Then he put the glass down and pointed at Finley's corpse. "What are we going to do about him?"

Ross shrugged. "There's no natural law here, so he started shooting with a shotgun. However, it's a tradition here that you pay some money to bury whoever you kill.

You know, for the funeral. The bartender—he'll take the money."

Byron took out a ten-dollar gold coin and threw it on the bar. "He's not worth it," he said, looking at Finley's remains. "I want to stay and have some fun, but I'm exhausted. I've been riding for so long."

Byron said he was going to the hotel and walked towards the door. He looked at the bartender and told him to use the ten bucks he left to bury the fat man deep enough so he wouldn't smell. He left the bar smoothly, never showing his back to anyone.

Boulder Ross stayed at the bar with his whisky and saw another man come to him from the back table. He was much smaller than Ross, but he moved with graceful confidence that earned him respect. The smaller man praised the fighter. He called him a catamount. He agreed that he fought well. He said it was only Finley who got beat. He felt sorry for old Finley. He said the fighter's name was Byron. He wondered how it would be to fight him. He laughed and said it would be painful. He observed that the fighter was fleeing from something.

Ross nodded. "You're probably right. It was exciting. I think Byron could be helpful to us."

2

A MAN WHO KILLED, BECAUSE HE LOVED KILLING.

The room cost thirty-five dollars a night, and they had to pay extra for water to wash with. The owner prohibited women from entering the room unless they were her guests. The men agreed, even though they thought thirty-five dollars was too much for this shabby place. But it seemed to be the only option in town. He agreed and took out some coins, which he put on the counter. "I have a horse outside; will it be safe?" "For another dime, I'll store it in the stables." One more coin joined the others on the counter, and the owner turned and yelled at Tommy while hitting a dead bell. Soon, a skinny boy of about thirteen or fourteen came out of a side door and stopped at the counter. "Yes, Miss Kathleen," he said, panting. Kathleen looked at the boy slowly. "You were slow, she said. This man has a horse outside; take it to the stable and ensure it's well looked after." "I'll get my stuff first," Byron said, following the boy, who was already running to the front door. "Let the boy get it; he can take it. It will keep the lazy kid busy." "I'll do it," Byron said firmly. She wisely kept quiet after receiving a sharp look from Byron. By the time Byron got to the sidewalk, the boy Tommy was already by the horse, admiring it. "Wow, nice horse, mister." But it was the big rifle that caught the boy's eye most. Byron walked up to the boy, reached into his pocket, and tossed him a quarter. Tommy was so surprised that he almost dropped the coin, catching it at the last second. He opened his hand and looked at the quarter as if he had never seen one before, which might have been true. At least, not so close, right in his hand. Byron said the quarter was a little extra, so he would clean his bike and polish it. "Jesus, thank you, mister," Tommy said. "I'll give the saddle leather a good shine." Byron nodded, impressed. He began to remove his travel gear from the horse's back. There wasn't much of it, just a couple of saddlebags, a bedroll, and the rifle. The boy's curiosity remained high as Byron pulled the big Winchester out of its holster.

"Holy cow, I've never seen a rifle like that before,"

Byron spoke of the Continental model. Calibre: 05-75. The bullets are one hundred and fifty grains. It shoots far and hits hard. When the boy asked in a low and hesitant voice, he turned to return to the hotel with his bag over his left shoulder, bedroll under his left arm, and rifle in his right hand. "

Uh, who was the guy who shot Finlay?"

Byron turned to Tommy and gave him a long look that made the boy sweat.

"Let me give you some advice," he finally said. "If you want to live a long and healthy life, stop asking people questions like that." Byron turned and went through the hotel's front door, disappearing inside. Tommy stayed still for a few seconds, feeling the heat of his sweat, and then took a brush and started to rub down the horse. "Holy cow," he kept saying to himself, glancing at the quarter, which he still held tightly in his fist.

To his surprise, the room he was given was not as bad as he had expected, considering the hotel's appearance and Miss Kathleen's attitude. True, it wasn't spotless and had little furniture, but it was spacious, and the bed was nice and firm, which meant he wouldn't have to throw the mattress on the floor. There was a pitcher of water next to the not-too-cracked washbasin. Byron poured some water into the basin, took off his shirt, and started to wash. He had a hard, muscular chest, with some bullet and knife wounds here and there.

After he had washed his face, he started to secure the room for the night. His first move was to wedge the back of a chair under the door handle. He then placed a water glass on the chair so that if anyone attempted to move it during the night, it would drop silently to the floor. He propped his rifle against the wall near the bed's head. His pistol went under the pillow. He then removed his boots and trousers and lay on the bed with the single cover drawn only halfway up his body. It was a hot night.

Before falling asleep, he reviewed the day's events for a few minutes. He wasn't fond of random killing, but he guessed that if anyone deserved killing, it was likely Finlay. He didn't need to worry about the outcome. All in all, it had been a fruitful day. He had only been in town for an hour and had already met with Boulder Ross. After all, what was the reason he was here?

A few seconds later, he was asleep.

Byron was in a very light sleep, his senses alert for any noise. The glass stayed on the chair. His right hand remained half under the pillow near his pistol, and his feet were always ready to hit the floor. All in all, it had been a fruitful day. He had only been in town for an hour and had already met with Boulder Ross, which, after all, was why he was here. A few seconds later, he was asleep.

Byron was in a very light sleep, his senses alert for any noise. The next few days were days of relative inactivity for Byron—somebody who spent most of his time in the saloon where he had killed Finlay. Fortunately, the man seemed to have had few friends; no one tried to avenge him. There was, in fact, a little good-natured joking about the fight. It was that kind of town.

There were few people in the saloon. The regular clientele was centred around Boulder Ross and his cronies. Ross seemed to go out of his way to be friendly to Byron. Byron responded cautiously, but within a few days, he was drinking regularly with Ross.

Byron needed some help warming up to his sidekick, Dean Philips. He was a tiny man with quick, graceful movements, which might have added a certain amount of appeal to his personality had it not been for the crazed gleam in his dark, narrow eyes. Byron immediately compared Philips to a man who killed because he loved killing. And, as Byron discovered, when Philips killed, they usually chilled with a knife. Philips was very good with a blade; he could produce one and slip it into an opponent before the opponent was even aware that the knife was near. Philips always carried a knife positioned somewhere on his body, toward his back; it took a lot of work to tell just where.

One night, Byron saw him use it in earnest. A stranger, a big man, well-hung with guns and accustomed to using them, had come into the bar. It did not take long to realize that the man had a natural ability, and since Dean Philips was a relatively small man, the stranger began to needle him after downing a few glasses of the local whiskey.

For about half an hour, Dean appeared to take the stranger's escalating insults quite meekly. Finally, his face twitched into a strange, crooked smile, and he approached the larger man. "You know, stranger," he said in an amused voice, "you're the first man I've ever met who spits through his mouth."

It took a moment for the stranger's whiskey-drenched brain to register the insult, but when it did, he lunged at Dean, spewing garbled threats. Dean dodged him easily, then landed a kick between his legs. The stranger gasped in pain, then doubled over, clutching his crotch. Dean stood over him, grinning that eerie grin, barely a few feet away from the stranger, eyeing his hands.

"How long have you been playing with yourself, you ugly bastard?" The gunman, who was also the stranger, snapped out of it and straightened up, hissing swear words as his right hand reached for his gun. But Dean was quicker. He stepped forward smoothly inside the stranger's reach, placing his left hand on the other man's right wrist so he couldn't complete his draw. At the same time, Dean's other hand went behind his back and came back with a knife.

He stabbed the stranger's stomach. A trickle of blood was the only sign of the wound until the stranger's expression changed to one of horror. He groaned, letting go of his weapon and attempting to push Dean away. He shrieked in agony as Dean slashed his knife across his belly, spilling his innards. Dean backed away, pulling out the knife. A torrent of dark blood spurted from the gaping hole in the stranger's stomach. He bent over, his hands desperately trying to prevent his guts from falling out. He raised his head slowly, his face twisting in pain. Dean was still close by, smiling wickedly and holding the knife low.

The stranger attempted to speak but couldn't. He tried to move forward but tripped, howled, and threw up. He should have collapsed then, but he summoned some strength from his dying body and reached for his gun with his right hand. He knew he was doomed, but he wanted to drag Dean down with him to hell. The stranger's entire body shuddered as the knife went into him for the second time.

Dean's face was still smiling as he knifed the stranger over the heart again, stepping back to witness the end.

The stranger's body jerked as the second blow hit him. Pain twisted his face as he slowly drew his gun from its holster. The gun shook in his hand. He had no chance to aim at Dean. The barrel moved up a bit more but stopped there. A violent spasm seized the man's body, and he fell face down. His legs twitched a few more times, and then he was motionless. The smile never left Dean's face. He stepped in again, this time driving the knife into the stranger's chest, right over the heart, and then he stepped back to watch the final act.

The stranger's entire body shuddered as the knife went into him for the second time. Dean's face was still smiling as he knifed the stranger over the heart again and stepped back to witness the end. The stranger's body jerked as the second blow hit him. Pain twisted his face as he slowly drew his gun from its holster. The gun shook in his hand. He had no chance to aim at Dean. The barrel moved up a bit more but stopped there. A violent spasm seized the man's body, and he fell face down. His legs twitched a few more times, and then he was motionless.

The bar had been silent since the fight began. Bulldozer finally spoke up. He chirped, "Damn it, Dean, you're making the undertaker a wealthy man with this kind of behavior."

Dean giggled and said, "He should lower his prices then. Yeah. We deserve a discount."

That was the end of it. As far as Byron could tell, the town seemed lawless, which might have spared him some trouble over Finlay's death. Dean Philips had carved a niche for himself. And by all of them, including Boulder Ross. He wished he could leave this place, maybe after getting rid of the local scum. But he had to stay. He had a reason to be here, and Boulder Ross was part of it.

One night, he found out that things were moving forward. Upon returning to his old hotel room from the saloon, he discovered that someone had searched it while he was away. It wasn't too obvious, but Byron had clever ways of detecting if someone had messed with his stuff, like the size and position of things or the presence of cobwebs. The signs indicated that he had a visitor.

Byron checked his bedroll and pulled out a wrinkled piece of paper that differed from where he left it. He glanced at the paper and noticed the fancy print. The words "United Martial" curled on top. Below that was an image of a single eye that never closed, and under it was the slogan, "We Never Sleep." The wanted poster offered five hundred dollars for Byron, who was on the run for robbery and murder. Byron smiled and put the wanted poster back where it was.

Good. They fell for it.

He noticed a curious glint in Boulder Ross's eyes the next day. Byron spent that morning, as usual, drinking terrible whisky at the saloon. But he entered the stable behind Miss Kathleen's Hotel in the afternoon. Tommy jumped up while lying on the hay; his fear was relieved when he saw that it was not Miss Kathleen, his boss, his tormentor, who had walked in but Byron, his benefactor.

"Hey, Tommy," Byron said. "Is the harness mender still hanging around town?"

"Yeah, sure, today only, Mr. Byron."

"Okay, I need to fix the side latches on my saddlebag."

"Oh, hell, Mr. Byron. I'd be happy to do it for you."

Byron gave the boy a puzzled look. Tommy flushed.

"It's not like that, Mr. Byron. You don't have to pay me anything at all."

Byron smiled. "I still owe you a quarter, Tommy, for how you've been looking after my horse here, keeping it safe and shiny," he said, tossing the boy a quarter.

Despite Tommy's recent denial of wanting money, his hands moved instinctively and caught the coin in the air. He held it awkwardly.

"I'll take that saddlebag over to the—"

He wanted to do it himself so he could tell him what he needed. And it would give him a break from that foul saloon. Byron grabbed the saddlebag and walked out of the stable, barely noticing the admiring gaze that followed him.

Damn it, kid, he thought sourly. Find some better role models.

According to Byron, the shop and owner were located on the outskirts of town. He roamed the countryside, fixing harnesses at remote ranches. Byron was taken aback. It seemed like he returned to town once a week to squander his scant earnings at the saloon rather than to find any customers here. The city was a dead end for businesses. Whatever purpose it might have had for existing here, it had long since disappeared. The surrounding land was pretty barren, just slightly better than wasteland. It was surrounded by rough hills on all sides. Maybe the only thing that kept it alive was a dependable hideout. Combined with its distance from the law, that drew men like Ross and Dean Phillips. And Byron.

The shop owner had been leaning on a log, drinking rotgut from a half-full bottle. Byron threw him the saddlebag. Byron's explanation of his desired action finally caught the apparent harness fixer's attention. He was a man of average height, hardened by years of roaming a cruel land. He always had the same amount of stubble on his face, as if it never got any longer. He was not a remarkable man—unless you saw his eyes, which were a piercing gray color. He normally kept his eyes low, but he raised them to Byron this time.

"Gardiner is wondering what you're up to. You haven't sent a report in more than a week."

"Tell him to buzz off. He went through my stuff."

"Yeah? Did he see the poster?"

"Yeah. A few days ago. He must have had a blast. It was a first-class piece of work. As real as they come."

"Sure. Real enough to maybe lure some moron to shoot me for the five hundred dollar bounty."

"Well, that's the price we pay for this wonderful, fun job, right?"

"I suppose. So, any updates? Any more thefts?"

"No. But Ross is still around, right?"

"Yeah. But we don't know if he's in on it."

"He better be. He's the only lead we have."

"A thin one."

"God, he's a vicious piece of work. What a bastard he is! That nickname, Boulder?"

"Yeah. He deserved it. They say he likes to smash men to death with his fists and feet until they're a bloody pulp."

"Dean Phillips is with him."

"No way!" the harness fixer exclaimed, shocked. "We had no clue."

"He's a weird-looking freak."

"Yeah," Byron said, remembering the man Phillips had killed. "I wish I could go in there and send them to St. Pete for some shooting practice. Do you want to join me? We'd be doing a favor to the world."

"No. They must stay alive until they can give us what we want."

"That's easy for you to say. You don't have to deal with those jerks every day."

The harness fixer stared at his dirty, ripped clothes and coarse hands.

"I'm not living the good life either. My mom didn't want her son to be a wandering hobo."

Byron grinned.

"Many mothers have to cope with failure."

"Like yours?" the harness fixer also grinned.

"Yeah. She never understood where she went wrong."

"I think that's fine, so what's next?"

They exchanged a silent understanding, and then the harness mender asked, "How do I explain to Gardiner?"

Byron shrugged. "Just tell him to stay calm. If an opportunity arises, it might happen very quickly. We're up against a very tricky group. They're suspicious of everyone. You just keep close to town. As close as you can without arousing anyone's curiosity. I'll let you know."

"Yeah. And take care of yourself. That way, we won't have to meet too often."

The harness mender nodded. Byron turned and walked away towards town and the saloon, where he didn't have to leave the only person in the area who would support him if things went wrong: Christopher Gardiner, the boss's brother.

3

JACKSON HOLE BADLANDS

Ross's job offer caught Byron off guard. He had expected more conversation and negotiation before getting to the proposal. At a bar, Ross approached him and asked if he wanted to make a lot of money. Byron was open to the idea but wanted to know more about what he had to do. Ross said that he expected Byron to do what he does best, which didn't include working. He also warned that the job would be dangerous, but the payout would be high. Byron was impressed by the potential earnings but wanted to hear more details. However, Ross insisted that he had to decide immediately without thinking it over. If Byron said no, he suspected Ross and his associates would harm him. So, he agreed to the job and prepared to leave with Ross and Dean Phillips.

During the journey, Byron asked for more information about the job, but Ross told him that he would reveal the details once they arrived at their destination. Dean Phillips made a comment, but Ross shut him down. Byron thought that Ross wasn't the one behind the planning because he didn't seem like someone who could plan anything. It was a long ride and distance, but they covered it in a single day. Still, by the time they made camp that night, Byron figured out they were probably heading for Wyoming's Jackson Hole country. That made sense. Jackson Hole Badlands lay between the Gros Ventre, French for "the big belly," and the Tetons. The Tetons were christened by grizzled, worn-out explorers from France. Their first thought upon seeing the majesty of that beautiful mountain range was of "Les Trois Tétons," the tallest of the three peaks, translated from French to "the big tit," a mountain range in the state of Wyoming. It was a natural haven for outlaws and desperados of all kinds, a place way out in the middle of nowhere, so isolated that it was hard to tell where you were—an intensely private place.

Byron could tell when they were nearing their destination. Late in the afternoon of the second day, Ross and Phillips, who had been riding pretty much without saying a word, became more animated.

"It's about time we had another payday," Phillips chirped. "The undertaker is eating up all my cash."

Ross laughed. "We'll have to do it for him someday this year—get back our money."

"Then who would bury the bastard? We need him, even if it's only to keep down the stink."

Cheered by this gentle trend in the conversation, Byron rolled his eyes morosely. He had been doing his best to track where they were going, although he suspected Ross had led them into the Badlands by a rather roundabout route. The countryside was ragged—a broken land with numerous canyons winding between barren buttes—a land so little traveled that there were few established trails. A man would need to know where he was going, and on top of that, he would need a lot of trailcraft to get there. It looked as if Ross might be lacking that trailcraft.

He and Phillips began to argue about their direction.

"It lies over that way, I tell you," Phillips insisted.

"Ah, shut up, Dean," Ross grumbled. "You can't find your way out of the front door."

Nevertheless, Ross looked worried. He led the three in broad sweeps, looking anxiously for landmarks. When Phillips finally let out a whoop and spurred his horse, Byron considered calling off the venture due to their lost location.

"By God!" Phillips yelled. "Forward!"

He vanished in an instant. Byron spurred his horse to a faster pace, and then he spotted a thin crack in the side of what had looked like a solid rock wall a moment ago. Ross gestured to the crack, telling Byron to go in through it. Byron paused for a second, not liking the idea of having the other man behind him in such a narrow space, but he knew he had no choice, so he went in.

The entrance was very tight, but it soon widened. A second later, Byron entered a small natural arena, an opening in the rock about two hundred yards across, with high stone walls. Byron doubted there was any way to reach the top of these cliffs from the outside. This was the most secure hideout he had ever seen.

They were not the first ones to get there. Several horses were roaming, unsaddled, near a pool of water from a small spring that poured a clear stream from a few yards up one of the rock walls. A man with a rifle suddenly appeared from behind a rock. His face relaxed when he saw Ross and Phillips, then tensed when he did not recognize Byron.

"Who the hell is that?" he asked Ross.

"A new guy. Don't worry about him."

The other man shrugged. "We'll see what the boss thinks of that."

Byron, Ross, and Phillips removed their saddles and started making food. They hadn't eaten much on the way and were starving. While he ate, Byron observed the men around him. If he had doubts about what Ross had offered him, he had none now. This was the most vicious-looking bunch he had ever seen—robbers and murderers, all of them. Nine men were present, including himself, Ross, and Phillips. A large force matched the robberies that had happened so far. They always rode in with many men, struck hard and fast, overcame any opposition, and then rode out as quickly as they had come in, loaded with loot. Ross had not lied. This was indeed an opportunity to make a lot of money—if a man survived.

Byron noticed that the men did not seem to know each other well. Someone else had recruited all of them. Smart. Tracing the others through one captured individual would pose a significant challenge. Byron began to recognise the indications of a brilliant mind behind all this, a fact that did not come as a surprise given the precision of the raids. It was also not surprising that Ross, despite displaying some cunning, did not possess a high level of intelligence. The few who had survived described the leader of this group as refined, clever, and cruel—a masked man.

It was almost dark when the leader showed up. He rode in through the thin opening on a big black horse, masked, wearing dark, expensive clothes, heavily armed, and clearly in charge. His eyes quickly scanned the whole arena. Byron was immediately noticed.

"What the hell is this man doing here?" he demanded, his voice sharp as a whip.

Ross quickly stepped forward. "It's okay, Boss," he said quickly. "I brought him."

The man stayed on his horse, looking down at Ross. "Did you bring him?" he asked incredulously. "Did you meet a stranger here?"

"I checked him out well, Boss. And you know we lost Jimbo last time, so we were one man short, and I thought—"

The Boss moved his eyes from Byron to Ross. "If I wanted you to think," he said coldly, "I would have told you. Didn't I make it clear that I'm the only one who chooses new men, and only me, and that's the only way we can prevent any of this from coming back to haunt us? Didn't I tell you that?"

"Yes, Boss. That's what you said, Boss. But I've made sure about this one. He's got a price on his head, and he's good with a gun."

"I don't give a damn if he's another Jesse James," the Boss said coldly. "I don't know a thing about him, and that's what counts to me. Who the hell are you, mister?" he asked, looking at Byron.

Byron felt the impact of the other man's eyes. They were a bright blue, contrasting with the dark mask that hid his face, and they drilled into Byron like no other eyes ever had. He knew he had to satisfy this man, who was likely nearing the end of his patience.

"I'm Byron," he said briefly. "I can also shoot."

The other man kept staring at him. Byron didn't flinch. Finally, the other man nodded.

"Fine," he said. "It's done. You're in. You can ride with us, but if you screw up in any way or make me dissatisfied with you, you're dead. Understand?"

Byron nodded. The Boss got off his horse and headed towards the fire.

"I need some food," he said sharply.

One of the men by the fire moved quickly and pointed to the stew pot over the flame. These men were hard, but when this unknown Boss gave an order, they obeyed it with remarkable speed. Byron thought he must be quite a man, able to build such discipline in this bunch. Even Ross, who was as murderous and independent as any man Byron had ever met, had been on edge when the Boss confronted him a few minutes ago. The only one who seemed to care less was Dean Phillips. But then, Byron thought, Phillips was a special case—a man so obsessed with killing that he noticed nothing else.

While the Boss was eating, Byron mingled with the other men. It soon became clear from their conversation that "The Boss" was the only name they called him by. He was a medium-sized man, perhaps slightly on the tall side, with a slim, muscular build. But it was not his physical presence that one noticed; it was the force of his personality, the hard, relentless strength that radiated from him. Once those frosty blue eyes fixed on someone, it was hard to think, let alone act.

The Boss got up from the fire, wiping his mouth on an expensive handkerchief. He had money, Byron decided. He must have grown up with it.

"Gather round," the Boss called out.

The men drifted towards the fire. When they formed a ring around him, the Boss said flatly, "We're hitting a mine this time. It's payday, and they've got a big workforce, which means a lot of cash. There's maybe a hundred thousand dollars to be paid out, most of it in gold. We ride in fast, wipe out any opposition, take the money, and then ride out as quickly as we rode in. We split the money as usual and then split up. Any questions?"

Ross was the only one to speak up, possibly because he was still upset about the Boss's treatment of him and wanted to express his feelings.

"Which mine are we hitting?" he asked.

The Boss looked at Ross for several long seconds.

"You amaze me," he finally said. "You know that, except for me, none of us are supposed to know the target until we're ready to strike. You know we do it this way so that no one can blab and spoil our plan before we've even started. So why the hell are you asking, Ross?"

"Well, I forgot."

"Now, let's get some sleep, and then we ride."

Byron saw the sullen look on Ross's face as the men went to their bedrolls. But he also saw that Ross held his tongue. Byron went to his bedroll with the others, trying to get as close as possible to the Boss without attracting too much attention. He tried to see beyond the mask, to imprint the other man's features in his memory, searching for some distinctive traits to make future identification easier. He couldn't look away from those penetrating blue eyes that suddenly fixed on him.

"I'm grateful," Byron said, thinking it was best to say something. "I'm glad you let me join this." The boss confronted him. "Don't forget what I said before. You're a gorier if you make me doubt you even a bit." Byron nodded. The boss walked away and went to his bedroll, but even though he lay down, Byron suspected that the other man wasn't sleeping. As the light dimmed, the sound of snoring echoed in the crisp, dry air—a scene that looked peaceful but was a precursor to theft and killing.

4

NOT PLANNED TO JOIN A RAID WITH OUTLAWS

They left shortly after midnight. The Boss had difficulty getting most of the men out of their sleeping bags as they swore and grumbled, but Byron was eager to get going. It was a beautiful night with a clear sky, as it often was during this season. There were no artificial lights to dim the stars, which filled the sky with dazzling splendour, and the Milky Way was a bright band of glittering light. The moon had not yet risen, but the light from the stars was enough to guide the ten men through the barren terrain.

Byron was not pleased with the situation. He had not planned to join a raid with outlaws. His job was to find them, especially their leader, and then lead a team to take them down. Like the harness mender, Byron was a long-time agent of the Pilkington National Detective Agency, working undercover. The wanted poster was a fake, made by his employers to give him credibility among the outlaws. However, his employers had widely distributed the poster to enhance its believability. When he told the harness mender that some bounty hunter might try to claim the reward for his head, Byron was not joking. If only he could have sent a message to the harness mender. But the Boss had planned everything carefully, making that impossible. For now, he had to play along with the role he had created—that he was a criminal. Eventually, he would seize the first opportunity to kill the Boss.

They rode all night. Byron had to admit that the Boss was good at keeping the men in line, making them move fast, and, most importantly, preventing them from fighting each other. They were a violent group, as much a threat to each other as they were to the law. The moon rose early in the morning, casting a pale light over the rough landscape. They could move faster now, and the Boss urged them on. "You will pay for all this discipline someday," Byron thought. They were not men who enjoyed receiving orders but had to comply with the

Boss's instructions. If they did not, the consequences would be severe.

As the darkness lifted and the eastern sky began to glow, the sun soon rose, giving the weary men some cheer—until the day became hot. The swearing and complaining grew louder. Finally, at noon, the Boss ordered a break, and the men gladly dismounted and looked for shade. But the Boss made them take care of their horses first.

"You'll need them to escape," he said. "If they're not in good condition, you could end up dead or in prison."

Byron was increasingly impressed by the Boss's sense of organisation and leadership. He wondered if he had ever been in the Army—or if he still was. The way he sat on his horse, upright and alert, suggested a cavalry background. Byron would have loved to know more about the man.

After an hour's break, they continued, but the Boss told them to stop when they started to see some cabins here and there. They hid for the rest of the day in a small ravine. Most of the men lay down to get some sleep, and the Boss instructed those who weren't sleeping to do so immediately. He warned them that it was going to be a long night.

They resumed their journey when the night was dark enough to conceal them. They kept riding until the Boss halted them at 1 a.m. As always, the horses came first for the Boss, and the men were secondary. He told them to settle and stay quiet since the mine was just beyond the hill. Once he ensured no one could spot the camp, he summoned Boulder, Ross, and Byron to scout. He had them survey the area on foot, even though they hated walking. For the horses to be useful, the terrain had to be more rugged and steep. At last, they reached the top of the stony peak, where the Boss showed them the mine about half a mile away. The mine had a night shift and a day shift working, and the Boss intended to strike right after the day shift went underground.

He drew a crude map of the mine's surroundings using the moonlight. He displayed a remarkable knowledge of the payroll and the mine's workings. Byron was curious about how he got this information. The Boss led Byron and Ross back to the camp, satisfied with their scouting. He told the two men to get some rest; they would leave at sunrise.

Byron went to his bedroll, which he had placed under the dark shade of a huge rock, hoping to sneak out at night and warn the mine workers. He noticed that Phillips had placed his bedroll close to his own. Phillips was lying in his bedroll, but he was not sleeping. Byron smiled at him.

"The Boss said so," Phillips remarked.

The Boss had designated a man to monitor Byron closely, and Phillips did not attempt to hide his involvement. Byron and Phillips had always disliked each other. Byron despised Phillips and did not care if he knew it. Phillips felt the same way about Byron. So, there was little hope of escaping to alert the mine about the attack. Byron slept as much as he could, waking up occasionally to see if Phillips had fallen asleep. Maybe he did sleep sometimes, but Phillips seemed to wake up every time Byron moved, his teeth gleaming in that same weird, mocking grin.

The Boss woke them just before dawn. They had a few minutes for a quick cold breakfast, then they got the horses ready, tied their bedrolls and guns, checked their weapons, and finally, it was time to go. The Boss divided the men into three groups, each taking a different path to the mine. The Boss had chosen the paths the previous night, selecting each one for its cover.

Everyone was looking at the safe. His meticulous and comprehensive work had allowed the bandits to reach the mine undetected, all at the same time. Things started to move fast.

"You and you," the Boss said to two men, "cover the entrance to the mine."

He ordered two more to cover the other direction. Another man was told to watch the horses.

"Sorry for missing it," the man said.

The Boss replied dryly, "Don't miss it again; it could be your last chance."

"I'm just so nervous that I'll mess up again," the man admitted.

The safe was what everyone was focused on, but Byron looked around the room. He saw something he hoped the others hadn't noticed. Partly hidden, the other clerk was slowly moving his left hand towards a thick cord that ran from the ceiling down the wall near a desk. The cord was equipped with a wooden handle. Byron saw the man's fingers reach for the handle. Byron knew how the cord worked. He tried to move and block the clerk but was too late.

The clerk by the safe had already obtained the combination when the safe door opened. This time, the clerk by the wall grabbed the cord's handle and pulled hard. Outside, a whistle started to scream.

The Boss turned around, his face furious. For the first time, Byron saw him lose his composure. "You stupid fool!" he yelled, pulling out his gun and shooting the clerk in the head.

The man fell back against the wall, his hands clutching his shattered head as he screamed. The cord swung, but the whistle continued to shriek like a wounded animal. The Boss returned to the safe. The other clerk, seeing his friend die on the floor with his brains spilling out, froze.

"Move!" the Boss yelled, pointing his smoking gun at the remaining clerk.

He ordered Boulder Ross to throw a large bag on the floor next to the safe. "Put all the money in it," the Boss commanded.

Byron could see inside the safe. It contained stacks of green bills and heavy bags of gold coins. He glanced at the man dying on the floor near him. If only he had his gun! The other clerk began placing money into the bag as the Boss ordered. The whistle continued to blare. Ross and Phillips were visibly scared. Then shots rang out from outside.

The man stationed at the door rushed in. "There are a lot of men out there!" he shouted.

"Hurry!" the Boss told the clerk, who had nearly finished filling the bag with money. The shots outside grew louder.

Another man, who had been outside, ran in. "We have to go!" he urged. "There are many men with guns out there. The night workers are coming out, and some of them have guns too."

The Boss instructed him, "Tell them to bring the horses to this side of the building." He then kicked the clerk and picked up the heavy bag. "Let's go," he said to the men with him. "Time to leave."

As he said this, the man at the door fell back, a bullet hole in his shirt. The Boss went to the window, took Byron's gun from his trousers, broke the glass with the gun, and fired all the bullets out the window. Angry and pained sounds emanated from outside. The Boss tossed Byron the empty weapon.

"Come on, let's go!" he shouted, drawing another gun and charging out the door.

Byron, Ross, and Phillips followed him outside, where a hail of bullets, screams, and smoke filled the air. A group of miners, hiding behind a building about fifty yards away, were firing at them. The Boss and his men returned fire. Byron realised how dangerous his situation was, standing there with the bandits and a gun in his hand. It was an empty gun, and he was not a bandit, but the miners didn't know that. They wanted to kill him too.

The bandits guarding the area took cover behind another building, firing accurately and providing cover for the man retrieving the horses. The horseman rode fast, lying flat on his horse, holding the reins of the other horses in one hand. His face was pale, but he appeared uninjured as he brought the horses to the building.

"Get on the horses!" the Boss ordered.

The survivors quickly mounted. There were nine of them, including the Boss. Someone shot the man in the office, leaving him dead. The bandits fled, with the Boss leading them towards a group of miners running to intercept them. The miners screamed, fired a few shots, and then ran away to hide.

Dean Phillips, laughing gleefully, dismounted, quickly knelt beside a fallen miner, cut the injured man's belt, and immediately remounted. The mine fighters, enraged by Phillips' actions, charged out of hiding, shooting wildly at the bandits. A bullet struck the man next to Byron. Byron heard the sickening thud of the bullet hitting flesh, followed by the man's short cry of pain. The injured man wavered on his horse, nearly falling, but another bandit rode close, holding him up and striking the injured man's horse with his reins, spurring the frightened animal to run.

They fled from the mine, riding fast, with some men shooting back at the mine fighters. Byron rode low on his horse, feeling bullets whizz past him. Being a marshal didn't help him now. Bullets didn't care who he was.

"They have horses!" Boulder Ross exclaimed. "They'll be after us soon."

Byron looked back. Sure enough, men were mounting horses at the mine.

"Oh no! They're going to catch us!" one of the bandits said.

"Be quiet and ride," someone else snapped.

But the injured man was slowing them down.

He was swaying on his horse, barely able to control it. The man who had helped him before tried to support him again, but it wasn't working. The Boss called out to stop briefly.

"No way," the man assisting the injured rider said. "Jack is my friend. I'm not leaving him behind, not while he's alive."

"Well, then, what now?" Dean Phillips asked, a crooked smile on his face as he drew his gun, intending to kill the wounded man.

Jack's friend pulled out his gun as well.

"Stop it!" the Boss ordered, putting his gun to Phillips' head. "No fighting among ourselves. How many times do I have to tell you?"

Phillips, still smiling, holstered his gun, but Byron noticed the dangerous glint in Phillips' eyes—a look that said he might shoot the Boss in the back when he wasn't looking.

Byron saw an opportunity; he was loading fresh bullets into his Remington. He had been running with the others since the mine, but maybe now he could stop the robbers and wait for the mine workers to catch up.

Just then, the injured man fell off his horse. His friend dismounted to help him, but at that moment, a group of riders appeared around a bend, about two hundred yards behind them. The men around Byron spurred their horses into a gallop, and they all charged down the road. Byron had no choice but to run with them or risk losing them.

Byron left the wounded man and his friend behind. The injured man struggled to his knees while his friend tried to help him up. But the riders closed in. The hurt man tried to conceal his gun, but they shot him repeatedly. Byron glanced back and saw it all unfold. Damn, those miners were quick with their guns. They didn't give the poor guy a chance to surrender.

Byron slowed his horse a bit, still watching. He saw the riders surround the injured man, who collapsed onto his back again. They lifted their guns, and six of them fired, the bullets slamming the hurt man into the dirt. Damn! They killed him while he was down! But why not? Byron thought. The miners had seen Dean Phillips dismount and steal a belt from one of their wounded comrades. They were enraged, seeking revenge. They didn't care about anything else, and with their money stolen, they wouldn't be enjoying themselves in town this week. The captured bandits would be lucky to meet a quick end; otherwise, they'd hang from a tree branch.

That ended any hope Byron had of working with the miners. As far as they were concerned, he was just another one of the men who had killed their friends and stolen their money. He couldn't tell them who he really was. He had to get out of there with the Boss and the others, or he'd be dead soon.

5

HE WAS TERRIFIED JUST LIKE THE REST

Byron quickly caught up with the others on his fine horse. They fled from the angry miners who were after them. Then he noticed something surprising. The boss, who had previously appeared so composed, was terrified just like the rest; he was riding erratically with his eyes wide open and his head close to his horse. After all, the jerk had a weakness. Byron's goal was to get out of this alive. He rode next to the boss.

"If you push the horses too hard, they'll collapse," Byron warned.

The boss looked at him sharply. "What do you suggest? That we slow down and let them catch us and hang us?"

"That's what will happen if we keep going like this. Their horses are fresh. We've been working for more than two days. We need to gain some time."

Dean Phillips joined them, talking tough. "Let's hear some ideas."

Byron looked around. The terrain was rough—not as harsh as the Jackson Hole area, but rough enough. He said, "We need to slow down; those rocks up there..."

About 500 yards ahead, the trail started to climb towards the heights where they had slept the night before. Huge rocks jutted out next to the point where the trail began to ascend.

"We'll put some men up there," Byron said, pointing at the rocks.

Boulder Ross understood right away. "Great idea. We'll shoot them off their horses."

Byron agreed, but he wanted to make sure that didn't happen. He was determined to save his own life, yet he harboured no intention of taking the lives of the men entrusted to his protection—the outlaws behind the rocks. Some of the horses were already very tired.

"We'll take most of the men ahead," Byron said to the boss. "Just leave me with two men with rifles. That should be enough to scare them away; they're miners, not shooters. You go slowly for about half an hour and then stop to rest the horses. The three of us should be able to hold them off for at least that long."

The boss observed him. "You seem to have calmed down. It's a good plan," he finally said. "But next time you have an idea, Byron, check with me first."

"Sure," Byron said, nodding. Praise the jerk. The important thing was to survive. The boss chose two men to stay with him. The boss silenced him with a cold look. Byron guessed that he had picked the most expendable men for the rear guard, which included him. That was fine with him. He wanted men he could control. He was glad he hadn't been paired with Ross or Phillips.

Byron and his two men quickly climbed into a high rock position, which ceased to be a battle, orchestrating

Adidas. They barely made it in time. The posse came around a bend about five hundred yards away. Byron placed the two men behind rocks with rifles pointed at the trail.

"Shoot their horses," Byron ordered.

"Why the hell for?" one of the outlaws inquired. He was a man with a rat face and bad teeth.

"Because they're easier to hit, moron. Do what I say."

The pursuers were now within four hundred yards. He raised his big Winchester, aimed down the long barrel, and fired. The first horseman's horse reared up, kicked the air, and fell hard, the rider barely jumping off in time to avoid being crushed. The animal's dying scream bounced off the rocks. By the time it had fallen, Byron had fired again. Another horse went down. The two men with him started shooting, the bullets kicking up dust about fifty yards in front of the posse. Jack Jones, rat-faced, smiled. A second later, he shot down a third horse.

"What the hell are you shooting with?" Rat-face asked.

"Winchester Centennial '05—'75. It shoots almost as far and as strong as Sharps."

Byron's next shot was missed, mainly because, seeing their friends fall, the horse riders below had the sense to hide and zigzag. Byron's partners got excited and started to shoot wildly, raising more useless dust.

"You fools, don't waste bullets," Byron snapped. "We may have to be here for a while."

Silence fell, except for the distant sounds of cursing from where the posse men had taken cover. Now they began to fire back at the rocks, but like Rat-face and his companion, their lighter-calibre rifles, mostly Winchester Seventy-threes, mostly chambered for pistol cartridges, could not quite reach their target. Byron knew they would try to work closer. He would use the larger range of his big Centennial to force them to keep their distance. The three horses lying in the open were enough of a warning. Byron noticed that one of them was still kicking feebly. With a headshot, he put it out of its misery.

"God almighty!" Rat-face half whispered under his breath.

It had now ceased to be a battle and had become a game of manoeuvre. The posse men were doing their best to work closer, circle behind the rocks, and cut off the defenders. Byron and his two men tried to keep them pinned down. Knowing that his advantage would eventually succumb to the posse's greater numbers, Byron began preparing his exit. Leaving the other two men to keep up a slow but continuous fire, he scoured the area, eventually finding several dead tree limbs straight enough for his purpose. Pulling out his Bowie knife, he lopped off any twigs or protuberances, cut the limbs down to about 6 feet, and then rolled them in the dirt to make them a uniform color.

When he returned to the others, he noticed a flicker of movement off to the left. Somebody was trying to flank them. He lay on the ground, carefully positioning his rifle. He fired a shot at a shadowy figure among the bushes below, heard a yell of fright, and fired again, kicking dust into the man's face. Now the man was running full tilt for cover.

"That should hold them for a while," Byron said. He looked up at the sun and calculated that they had already delayed the posse by more than half an hour. He pulled his two men back, then laid the sticks he had cut into place, pointing down at the flats below, hoping they would look like rifles.

"Okay," he whispered to the others. "Let's get our arses out of here, really quiet."

Initially, the two gunmen searched to determine if their sacrifice would allow the others to escape. They were more than glad to believe in it. The three of them slid down the backside of the rocks, took the reins of their horses, and quietly led them up the trail. They weren't mounted and were more than 100 yards away. Behind them, they could hear the posse men still firing an occasional shot.

"Good. The miners are making enough noise that it might take them a while to realise that no firing is coming back at them from the rocks. That may hold them for another 10 minutes or so," Byron said. "Let's make tracks, but try not to push your horses too hard."

They caught up with the others an hour later. They were riding along sedately, their horses looking rested. Byron's mount was still in pretty good shape; the other rocks had helped. The two men with him had shown themselves to be good horsemen; their mounts were in relatively good shape, too. The boss extracted a description of what had happened from Rat-face and his companion. He then nodded towards Byron.

"Good work."

"Thanks. Now, let's get lost." The boss nodded again, his expressionless face hidden behind the mask.

"Suppose you are sure as hell. I'm glad to oblige."

For the next few hours, Byron used every bit of cunning in him to shake himself and the others loose from the posse. He led the way upstream, only leaving the water when he determined that the terrain could conceal their tracks. They trailed a small horse for several miles, blending its tracks with their herd's, but a skilled tracker should be able to distinguish the animal's hoof marks from those of the unshod wild ponies. Byron eventually rode close enough to spook the herd, causing the animals to run off in all directions, which he hoped might confuse any trackers.

By nightfall, they sprawled on a high plateau, resuming their horse-riding attire. The boss was lying on his stomach, studying the trail below with large binoculars.

"I think you've done it," he called out to Byron to take a look.

Byron came over and took the glasses. Following the boss's pointed finger, he studied the line below. Yes, there they were, about a mile away—the posse, milling about in confusion at the point where the trail split five ways. He could imagine arguments flying back and forth between those men as each projected where the quarry had gone. Finally, they turned down one of the five trails leading directly away from where the bandits were hiding. Byron smiled.

"Yes. I figured there would be a choice."

"You mean you planned that, too?" the boss inquired.

"More or less. I noticed some hoof prints leading off in that direction. We were already above the main trail. It seemed sensible that they would follow the only tracks they could see. I didn't figure they had anybody with them good enough at tracking to realise those prints were over a day old."

Phillips's voice cut in, cool and mocking. "You're a real Indian scout here, boys."

Byron turned around and looked back at him. Phillips met his gaze for a moment, then casually looked away.

Someday, Byron promised himself, I'm going to chill that little bastard.

There was now little fear of further pursuit. The seven survivors of the mine raid pushed on towards their hideout in the Jackson Hole region. On the second evening of their flight, the men were exhausted and some of their horses nearly dead. Most men flopped onto the ground, too tired to spread their bedrolls. Now, the boss had firmly regained control and had instructed the guards to stand watch. Byron wondered what had brought on that strange panic at the beginning of their flight. There was a certain degree of instability in the boss's make-up. A strange man.

Byron offered to stand guard. The boss hesitated, then finally agreed.

"He trusts me now," Byron thought. "Why not? I saved his skin today."

The next morning, when a rested and eager group gathered around, the boss tossed his big canvas bag to the ground and knelt to untie the cords holding it closed. The bag had not left his possession since the terrified clerk in the mine office had stuffed it with money. The bag held more than thirty thousand dollars, and the boss counted out more than three thousand apiece to each man. His share was more than thirteen.

One of the men dared to complain about the size of the boss's cut. The boss's head came up, his cold, bright blue eyes pinning down the complainer. The boss's icy words hung in the air: "Good planning comes at a price. If you dislike our money division, speak up and leave."

The man hesitated, then nodded. Everyone knew that leaving this outfit meant facing a grim fate. But it wasn't just the complainer who resented the boss's hefty cut. Seeing the tension, the boss defused it by offering a thousand dollars each to Byron and the two men who had stayed behind to slow down the pursuing posse.

"Extra risks deserve extra pay," the boss stated crisply.

The fact that this danger bonus came from his share quelled the general resentment.

"Alright," the boss declared. "Let's part ways until next time."

The men scrambled to prepare for departure. Byron sensed an opportunity. If the boss left the hideout last, that would be the moment to strike. However, to Byron's surprise, the boss rode out early. Byron tried to find an excuse to follow him, but he failed. Ross and Phillips were already saddling up.

"Come on," Ross called out cheerfully. "Saddle your horse, and let's ride to town. We've got a fortune to spend."

Byron had no choice but to join them. When he left the hideout, there was no trace of the boss, no hint of his direction. His tracks merged with those of the other riders. Riding alongside Ross and Phillips, Byron concealed his curiosity. Yet during the long journey back to town, he used every ounce of trail wisdom to etch the hideout's location into his memory and scout for ambush spots. Notably, the first few miles offered only one viable route away from the hideout.

Byron's pulse raced in sync with the pounding hooves of his horse. The trail stretched ahead, a winding ribbon of dust and secrets. The gang's chosen route, the same path they'd tread during their daring raids, was now etched in Byron's mind. Valuable information, indeed.

Dean Phillips, that slippery provocateur, had become a thorn in Byron's side. His taunts, like venomous bites, pushed Byron to the edge.

"Arrest them now," a voice whispered in Byron's mind. He could draw his gun, declare them under arrest, and end this treacherous game. But the gang had already lost men on this raid. Two more losses would weaken their ranks significantly. Yet Byron knew the boss was the gang's nucleus—the pulsing heart orchestrating their criminal symphony. The enigmatic figure slipped through the shadows, leaving no trace. Without him, the gang would be a disjointed collection of desperate souls, their guns mere tools without purpose.

"Cut off the head," Byron mused.

The boss was no ordinary criminal; he was a mastermind, a chess player moving pieces across the board. Eliminate him, and the gang would crumble like a house of cards. The members would scatter, leaderless, their whispered loyalties fading into the wind. But how? Byron's fingers itched for his Colt, but he couldn't risk blowing his cover. The boss remained elusive, slipping away like smoke. Byron clenched his jaw. He wouldn't wait. Not anymore. The next opportunity to get a clear shot at the boss would be his moment.

The sun dipped lower, casting long shadows. Byron rode on, his determination burning hotter than the desert sun. The showdown loomed, and Byron's fate hung in the balance. Would he be the hunter or the hunted? Only time and a well-aimed bullet would decide.

6

TOO MANY DEAD BODIES

An hour later, back in town, Byron, freshly washed, dried, changed, and cleanly shaved, approached the weathered shack where the harness mender usually held court. The mender sat outside on a flat rock, his eyes squinting against the sun. As Byron drew near, the mender raised a lazy hand in greeting, then disappeared into the shack. He emerged moments later, holding Byron's mended harness, which he handed over.

"About time," Byron grumbled, accepting the bridle.

The mender settled onto his rock. "I finished it a couple of days ago," he replied. "But you weren't around to collect it."

Byron sat across from him. "Been out for a little ride," he said.

"Nothing to do with that mine payroll robbery, I hope?" the mender's eyes flickered.

"It just might," Byron responded.

"You were there?" The mender leaned forward.

Byron nodded slowly. "Too many dead bodies," he said. "We've got to stop those bastards."

Byron smirked. "Hard nut to crack," he said. "Their leader's smarter than hell; he plans every move down to the last detail."

"You've met him?" The mender's curiosity was evident.

"Yeah," Byron replied. "Wore a mask. None of his men know who he is. But we're close enough. I think we can bust them wide open."

They huddled, strategising for another twenty minutes. Finally, Byron decided it was risky to linger any longer. He picked up his harness and headed back to his hotel. The next few days would be a waiting game.

Meanwhile, Boulder Ross and Dean Phillips, the notorious bandits, departed town early the following day.

With a conspicuous lack of available women, they rode towards the nearest settlement, a place with a stable full of willing ladies to satisfy their needs. After an absence of over a week, Boulder Ross and Dean Phillips returned, their appearances revealing the toll of their escapades. The dwindling funds from the mine robbery were evident in their surly demeanour.

While they indulged in their vices, Byron had another clandestine meeting with the harness mender. One night, the mender materialised beside Byron—an unsettling abruptness that sent them both into a foul-smelling alleyway.

"I found it," the harness maker murmured. "Just as you described, there is only one way in or out."

"Will it work?" Byron asked.

"I don't see what else would," the mender's voice was low. "Wait for my signal." With that, he melted back into the shadows.

For several days, Byron didn't spot him around town—a near miss? The following evening, Boulder Ross approached him in the saloon, just a day after the harness mender had returned.

"Want to make more money?" Ross inquired.

Byron nodded. "Yeah."

"Good. There's a raid. We leave in an hour. Get your gear."

Now more trusted, Byron retrieved his belongings from his room. He swiftly filled his saddlebags, prepared his bedroll, and almost as an afterthought, hung his grubby shirt in the window frame. Knowing Miss Kathleen's lack of service, he was confident the shirt would remain untouched.

Byron, Ross, and Phillips set off, the wheels of their getaway wagon turning within the hour. As they rolled out of town, Byron made deliberate noise, hedging his bets by employing multiple methods to alert the harness mender. The shirt in the window might suffice, but then again, it might not. The stakes were high, and the game was afoot.

Byron's Calculations and the Ambush

The journey to the hideout followed its usual rhythm—a day and a half of travel. Byron's mind churned with calculations, envisioning the events unfolding behind him. If the harness mender had indeed seen his signal and understood that the gang was about to strike again, specific actions should be taken. The mender, acting on Byron's instructions, had personally scouted the land surrounding the hideout. Meanwhile, a sizeable contingent of U.S. marshals had been stationed within a day's ride of the hideout for the past week. The harness mender would swiftly reach the closest telegraph office, send out a message, and initiate the marshals' movement. Their mission was to ambush the bandits when they left the hideout. However, the timing was crucial. The marshals needed to reach the ambush site promptly.

Byron estimated they had just over eight hours since he left town with Ross and Phillips. It would take roughly 30 hours for the trio to reach the hideout, a few more hours for the rest of the gang to assemble, and then a night's rest before departure. A tight window of eight hours, give or take.

Byron, Ross, and Phillips arrived at the hideout on the second day as dusk settled. Surprisingly, many gang members were already present, and even more surprisingly, the boss awaited them. He shot Byron and his companions an irritated glance before focusing on the hideout's entrance.

"Where the hell are they?" he muttered, referring to the two missing men. "It's high time we got moving."

Byron, taken aback, asked, "Are we leaving right away?"

The boss's response was curt: "Yes. Within the hour. Does that bother you?"

It bothered Byron very much. If they left now, the ambushers wouldn't have enough time to settle in, as opposed to at night or in the morning.

"I was hoping we could get a little rest," he said to the boss.

"This isn't a knitting bee, Byron," the boss said testily. "Timing is of the essence in this operation. We will have to move out on schedule, whether we are all here or not."

The last operation had lost the men, and Byron spotted new faces. The boss had done some recruiting. If everyone showed up, there would be a total of ten men. There were too many men to handle by himself, and that would be his only alternative unless he could find some way to delay their departure.

He attempted to devise a practical strategy, possibly involving a significant horse or two, but he needed to figure out a way to carry it out without attracting attention. Of course, he could blame his horse, but then they'd simply leave him behind.

The two missing men arrived half an hour later. "Okay, mount up," the boss ordered. There was a great deal of grumbling as the men swung into their saddles; Byron was not the only one who had indicated a desire for some slack time. Byron had no choice but to go along with the others. To hang back now would cost him his life.

There was no ambush. He rolled past the ambush point without incident. All that Byron could do was ride at the rear of the little cavalcade and do his best to leave the broadest trail possible. The marshal's posse could follow the gang if he left enough signs. He knew they were carrying old Thomas Laird with them. Thomas had been a scout and tracker for the cavalry during the Indian campaigns. Before that, he had lived many years with various Indian tribes. Could Thomas follow a trail through land like this at night? It would be dark soon. They would ride until very late, according to the boss's haste.

The boss called a halt a little after midnight, more to rest the horses than the men. The stop was a short one—only two hours. Then they were on their way again, pushing on until an hour past dawn, when the boss led them into the shelter of a small wood overlooking a large town about a mile away.

"Rest up, boys," he said, pointing down towards the town. "I'll be down there in a while, robbing the bank."

The men gratefully dismounted, the more intelligent among them unsaddling their mounts, rubbing them down, then feeding them a small ration of oats—not enough to founder them but enough to give them energy if speed was needed later. This would likely occur once the boss had successfully robbed the bank. Like any good commander, the boss let the men know a little about the operation so they would feel a part of it.

"We have to hit the bank just as it opens," he explained. "They have a time lock on the vault, so hitting it earlier wouldn't be as good. I also happen to know that the local sheriff will be out of town this morning due to a request he got to investigate some stock shortages clear over on the other side of the county."

"We know who sent him that request," one of the men said with a grin.

The boss favoured him with a smile. "He'll never be able to navigate the channels effectively. Anyhow, I'll hit the bank hard and hit it fast. In and out in 15 minutes—that's the way I have it planned. Now, any questions?"

"Yeah," Byron said, cutting in more to slow things down than out of any genuine curiosity. He kept thinking of the marshals following behind on their trail, if indeed they were following. "How much cash do we figure there is in the bank?"

"About one hundred thousand dollars," the boss said coolly. Several of the men whistled. A hundred thousand dollars was one hell of a lot of money.

"Are you sure?" Byron asked.

"Yes, I'm sure," the boss replied, an acid edge to his voice. "I have ways of knowing."

Byron silently wondered just what those ways might be. The boss had anticipated how much there would be at the mine. He also knew some details about the inner workings of the mine office. Just who was he, anyway, that he could know these things?

They mounted up at precisely nine o'clock, all ten of them, and moved in a compact body towards the town. There was no point in slipping into town in small groups, unnoticed. The mask covering half the boss's face was enough of a giveaway. So, they rolled in boldly, walking their mounts until they were within sight of the town's inhabitants, and then, on the boss's orders, they all put spurs to their mounts and rushed the bank.

Here we go. In a meticulously planned operation, the gang positioned themselves strategically around the bank. Rifles and pistols gripped tightly, standing ready to thwart any attempts by the townspeople to defend their financial institution. The memory of the James-Younger gang's near annihilation by an enraged citizenry after their Minnesota bank heist weighed heavily on every bank robber's mind.

The remaining five men, including the enigmatic Byron, burst into the bank, brandishing their weapons.

"Up against the wall!" the boss barked, aiming his pistol at the customers. Wide-eyed and frozen, the customers hesitated. A gunshot echoed as the boss fired into the floor near a man's foot, sending splinters flying. The pain propelled the man to join another customer pressed against the wall, hands raised in surrender. Meanwhile, a clerk attempted to slip out the back door, but Ross swiftly shot him through the right leg. The wounded clerk writhed on the floor, cursing and howling, clutching his bleeding limb.

Inside the bank, the operation unfolded like clockwork. Three of the bandits moved from teller to teller, stuffing canvas bags with money. The boss and Dean Phillips herded the sweating, visibly terrified clerks and the bank manager towards the vault, the repository of real wealth. In less than 15 minutes, as the boss had specified, they amassed all the valuables worth taking.

"Everyone into the vault!" he commanded, gesturing towards the customers, clerks, and the trembling bank manager.

The manager's voice quivered: "But there's no air in there!"

The boss remained unfazed. "You'll stay outside while we lock them in. You know the combination. We'll ride away, and it's a good enough plan."

And so, with precision and audacity, the bank robbers executed their daring heist, leaving behind a stunned and captive audience within the vault.

The town would remember this day for years when desperation and criminal cunning collided in a high-stakes battle for fortune. The bank manager grappled with a harrowing choice: save his customers and clerks or ensure the gang's successful getaway. He stood beside the vault, wringing his hands, as the prisoners were herded inside. The boss slammed the heavy vault door shut and spun the dial, locking away the bank's riches.

"Don't open it until you hear our horses riding away," he ordered the manager, who nodded in mute agreement.

"Okay, let's hit the trail!" the boss shouted to his men. They strode towards the exit when the sudden sound of Byron's voice echoed from outside.

"Speed up!" the boss urged, racing for the door.

Once outside, they found their comrades crouched low beside the horses, firing down the street.

"What's happening?" the boss demanded.

"Some citizens," came the reply, "holed up in that hotel. They've started shooting at us. I think we hit one, which should keep their heads down."

"Good enough. Mount up!" the boss commanded. "We'll head out of town in the opposite direction."

A heavy barrage from two bandits strategically positioned near the bank slowed the hotel's rate of fire. Byron swung into the saddle beside the others, cursing inwardly. If only the boss hadn't meticulously planned every move, they could have infiltrated the gang's ranks. Meanwhile, the townspeople kept them disoriented with their gunfire from the old teller's office. But it wasn't unfolding that way. So far, not a single bandit had been hit—their accuracy was uncanny.

Byron watched as bullets tore into the building, shattering windows along the side of the whole story. Almost no one was firing back at them now. Their escape plan was simple: ride out of town in the opposite direction, with the boss leading. Suddenly, one of the bandits cried out in alarm.

"Jesus Christ!" he screamed, pointing towards a horde of heavily armed men thundering into town from the very direction the gang had hoped to avoid. Panic surged—their desperate escape was about to collide head-on with an unexpected and formidable force. Byron's U.S. Marshals Posse had arrived at last.

7

HEAVILY ARMED AND WELL-TRAINED MEN

Between fifteen and twenty heavily armed and well-trained men were making rapid advances. The boss, startled, flinched away from them, contemplating fleeing on his horse. However, in that direction lay the hotel, guarded by armed townspeople. Just as events seemed to turn against him, the boss displayed signs of panic and indecision. Initially, he sat rigidly on his horse, unsure of his next move. Then, losing control, he spun the animal in a complete circle, scanning in different directions. Adding to the chaos, the portly bank manager, previously unassuming during the robbery, suddenly emerged on the pavement, brandishing an enormous shotgun.

"Rob my bank, will you?" he bellowed, firing both barrels at the nearest bandit. He flung the man from his saddle, leaving his left side completely destroyed. With his weapon now empty, the bank manager wisely retreated to the relative safety of the bank to reload. Meanwhile, the boss regained his resolve, veering his horse into an alley next to the bank. Boulder Ross, Dean Phillips, and another man pursued him relentlessly. As the posse's gunfire intensified, saddles emptied around Byron. Several horses fell, and their wounded riders sought cover behind the fallen animals, desperate to return fire.

Byron's heart raced as chaos unfolded in the narrow alley. The boss and his armed companions charged ahead, desperate to escape. Byron urged his horse forward, fingers fumbling to draw his rifle from its sheath. But fate intervened—a searing impact slammed into his ribs, threatening to unseat him. Pain surged through his side, and warmth spread like wildfire. He'd been hit, likely by a stray bullet from the posse. Amid the relentless gunfire, the U.S. marshals couldn't afford precision. His duty was clear: evade the crossfire. Yet fear for the boss's escape held him back. Time slipped away, and now urgency propelled him.

Clinging to his horse's sturdy barrel with his legs and spurs digging in, Byron galloped after the fleeing bandits. Blood soaked his shirt, but determination fuelled his pursuit. With his left hand, he pressed hard under his right arm, desperate to stem the crimson tide. As he rode forward, Byron noticed the boss and a fellow rider about 100 yards ahead. The boss, struggling to maintain balance in the saddle, had evidently taken a hit. With effort, he regained his seat, aided by a companion riding alongside. Byron spurred his horse, determined to catch up.

Meanwhile, the fleeing bandits vanished into a labyrinth of buildings and equipment at the far end of the alley. Casting a quick glance behind, Byron observed the bandits blocking the alley mouth, fiercely battling the pursuing posse men. Unbeknownst to them, this struggle inadvertently shielded the others—the boss, Ross, Phillips, and the men who had abandoned them. Byron knew he couldn't count on assistance. Urging his horse onward, he rounded a corner and glimpsed the four men ahead, still riding hard. They were leaving the last buildings behind, heading towards a wooded area about a mile from town. Byron doubted that the posse men could spot them amidst the chaos.

Byron's breaths came in ragged gasps as he finally caught up with the others within the shelter of the dense woods. The adrenaline that had fuelled his desperate ride was now waning, replaced by a searing pain radiating from his right side. His arm hung limp, almost useless.

"Byron!" Ross's voice cut through the haze. "You made it out."

"Yeah," Byron rasped, his left hand still pressed against his injured side. The pain was sharp, but he couldn't afford to collapse now.

"He's hit too," Phillips interjected, concern etching his features.

"Not too bad," Byron murmured, though doubt gnawed at him. He edged closer, eyes fixed on the boss—the masked man who had orchestrated this chaos. Blood stained the entire back of the boss's shirt, a grim testament to the severity of his wound.

Dean Phillips dismounted, signalling to Boulder Ross. "Help me get him off the horse," Phillips urged, determination in his eyes. The stakes were high, and they couldn't afford to lose their leader now. The pursuit had taken its toll, but they were still in the game. Byron clenched his teeth, ready to assist. The woods held their secrets, and survival demanded every ounce of their resolve.

With the help of the fourth man, they got the boss dismounted. He grunted with pain, his eyes half-glazed, but he seemed to be doing his best to cooperate. Phillips took out his knife and cut away the boss's shirt. There was a small, pulsing hole high up on the wounded man's back, slowly welling blood. Working with amazing speed, Phillips cut up part of the bloody shirt for compression, pressed it against a wooden board, then wound the rest of the shirt in long strips around the boss's body, holding the compress tightly in place.

Phillips motioned to Byron, who was still sitting on his horse. Byron slid to the ground, grunting at the pain that had cost him. Phillips tore at his shirt, examined his ribs, and found nothing much.

"Bullets struck you at an angle and bounced off your ribs. I suppose it hurts like hell, but it isn't likely to kill you."

Ross and Byron stood near the wounded boss, who slumped against a tree, his back propped up by a rock. The situation was dire—the boss had taken bullets, and they were still lodged inside him. His survival was in jeopardy, and the decision weighed heavily on their minds.

"He's another story," Byron murmured, his gaze fixed on the injured man. "Bullets are still in there. He could check out on us. Either way, he's going to slow us down. What do you say? Should we take him with us or leave him behind?"

Ross hesitated, furrowing his brow.

"We ought to take him along," he finally said. "He knows who we are. If they get their hands on him, we could be dead meat."

Phillips shook his head.

"Not if he isn't alive to talk," he insisted. "But consider this, Ross: we've been raking in money working with that man. If he stays healthy, we could make a lot more."

Phillips's frustration surfaced.

"He isn't making as much this trip," he groused. "When he got hit, he dropped those two big money bags he was carrying. Now we're left with just the two little ones."

The tension in the woods was palpable. Loyalties clashed with survival instincts, and the stakes couldn't be higher. They had to decide: protect their lucrative partnership or cut their losses and ensure their own escape. The shadows of the trees bore witness to their deliberations.

"That's why we've got to keep him alive. Souls, we can get more," Byron asserted, his voice strained. The wounded boss slumped against the tree, his life hanging in the balance. The bullets still lodged inside him threatened to tip the scales towards death.

"Well, okay," Ross conceded, his gaze fixed on the injured man. "But if he looks like he isn't going to make it…"

The notion of honour among thieves seemed laughable now. It would have been simpler for Byron if they could just dump the boss right there, but circumstances didn't align. Not at this moment. Byron's desperate hope rested on the posse men catching up soon. Despite his own injuries and the odds stacked against him, he might disrupt the surviving gang members long enough to ensure their capture or demise. Once again, he found himself tagging along, a reluctant participant in this dangerous game.

Phillips had bound up Byron's wound, the pain now throbbing relentlessly—a sign that he was still alive. He flexed his right hand's fingers, contemplating how they would handle his trusty .45's recoil. Surely the posse would be hot on their trail. Yet, hour after hour, they rode, and there was no sign of pursuit. Byron's memory flickered back to their path through the stockyards. The churned ground there bore witness to their desperate flight, and the trees' shadows concealed their secrets. The stakes remained high, and survival demanded every ounce of their resolve.

As they pressed onward, the ground bore witness to their desperate flight—a mass of hoof prints, both from horses and cattle. Even old Thomas Laird would struggle to discern their sign amidst this chaotic churn of tracks. Then, as evening descended, rain poured down—a relentless deluge that threatened to erase their very existence. Byron glanced back along the trail, watching their tracks vanish under the force of the downpour. Boulder Ross, ever resourceful, veered them off the main trail and into the mountains. The likelihood of tracking them had significantly decreased.

The boss, wounded and weakened, faced a gruelling ordeal. Phillips called several halts, each time helping the boss dismount. He checked the bandages, replenished water, and tended to the man's needs. The boss, now only half-conscious, made no protest when Phillips removed his mask to offer water. Studying the boss's unmasked face, Byron noted that he could be considered a good-looking man. The weariness in his eyes, partly glazed, softened his regular, strong features, revealing a man who had lost his bearings in this treacherous pursuit. He thought the boss had guts. Every time they hoisted him back into the saddle, he maintained his grim determination.

They rode throughout the afternoon and into the night. Byron, growing somewhat light-headed from a lack of blood, lost track of time. He hardly knew what was happening when the little band of tired men finally ended its journey. He vaguely recalled receiving assistance in a small, dirty, and seemingly abandoned house. He observed the spread-out bedroll on the floor, sank down onto it, and fell asleep moments later.

He awoke at dawn, aching fiercely on his right side. He lay still, eyes only half open, and in the dim light, Boulder Ross and Dean Phillips bent over a form stretched out on the cabin's only bed. Turning his head slowly, Byron saw that it was the boss. Ross and Phillips were speaking in low voices, but Byron was able to make out what they were saying.

Phillips insisted that the bullets had to come out, or else the boss would die.

"So take it out," Ross replied.

Phillips snorted.

"That'll kill him, for sure. I'm not a doctor."

A weak but still commanding voice emanated from the bedridden figure. Byron watched as the boss's head slowly turned towards Ross and Phillips.

"I need a doctor. Fetch one, and you'll each receive five thousand dollars."

Ross and Phillips exchanged glances, their eyes alight with the promise of money. Ross hesitated, then looked back at the boss and nodded.

"Okay," he finally agreed. "There's a town about half a day's ride from here. I'm pretty sure they have a sawbones. I'll find him and bring him here."

"How will you convince him?" Phillips inquired.

Ross's hand hovered near the holster on his side.

"I'll think of a way," he replied cryptically.

A few minutes later, Ross disappeared, leaving Phillips behind to tend to the wounded boss. The rain continued to fall, washing away their tracks, and the woods held their secrets as they waited for help—or perhaps betrayal—to arrive.

Byron's resolve wavered as he stepped outside, meeting Phillips's gaze. The other man who had escaped with them lay sprawled on his bedroll, fast asleep. Byron strained to recall his name—Tate, that was it. A recent addition to their ragtag group, Tate struck Byron as rather dim-witted, brutal, a bully, and a coward. Tate blinked owlishly at Byron, oblivious to the brewing tension. Perhaps now was the opportune moment to act—to disarm Tate and then slip into the cabin, where Phillips remained alone with the wounded boss. Surely the boss's injuries rendered him incapable of resistance.

Yet Byron's own right arm protested every movement. How effective could he be? If he made even the slightest noise while disarming Tate, Phillips would pounce. Perhaps waiting for Ross's return was the wiser course of action. Byron needed Ross—someone he could trust.

And so, guided by the sound of running water, Byron followed a small, clear stream. He peeled away the remnants of his shirt, unwinding Phillips's bandages. The rain continued to fall, washing away their tracks, and the woods held their secrets as Byron grappled with his choices.

Byron examined his wound—a gruesome gash along his side, tracing the path of the ribs. While not immediately life-threatening, it felt as if a rebel yell had cracked through him when a bullet ricocheted off his body. Any rapid movement, even breathing, proved agonising. Could he even hold a pistol in this state? It would be better to postpone any showdowns until he regained strength.

He dipped his shirt into the icy water, wincing as the sting shot through him. Gritting his teeth, he meticulously sponged away the dried blood until he was satisfied that it was clean. Then, with aching limbs, he rummaged through his saddlebags. A clean shirt awaited him, along with some worn pieces of cloth. He fashioned a fresh bandage from the cloth, securing it tightly around his wound. Finally, he donned the clean shirt, feeling a semblance of relief—but exhaustion weighed heavily upon him. The woods held their secrets, and the rain persisted, washing away their tracks as Byron fought to survive.

Byron's efforts to tend to his wound had left him drained. Undoubtedly, he had lost a significant amount of blood the previous day. When he returned to the cabin, he retrieved his bedroll with his left hand and carried it outside into the sun. He laid down on a bed of pine needles, spreading them out, allowing the warm sun to soothe his wounded side and ease the tension in his muscles. After about half an hour, exhaustion claimed him, and he drifted into sleep.

Byron groaned, simulating the disorientation of waking.

"Jesus," he grunted, teeth clenched as he pushed himself upright.

"Stiffening up a little, isn't it?" Phillips quipped, a grin dancing on his lips.

Despite Byron's struggle, Phillips made no move to assist him as he regained his feet. The woods held their secrets, and the sun continued its relentless journey across the sky as Byron rested, caught between survival and weariness.

8

THE NECESSITY FOR AN ANAESTHETIC.

Boss returned to the cabin just before dusk, accompanied by the doctor. The physician's demeanour didn't exude enthusiasm for this particular house call; it was evident that Ross had coerced him at gunpoint. The doctor, a middle-aged man with a competent appearance, stepped inside the cabin to meet the boss. Any reservations or grudges he may have harboured vanished, replaced by a sense of urgent professionalism. Addressing Ross and Phillips, the doctor's tone was sharp: "This man should have sought medical attention long ago."

With a snicker, Phillips responded, "Well, Doc, we weren't sure if any doctors were part of the posse."

Undeterred, the doctor began issuing orders, met with some hesitation from Phillips and Ross. Byron intervened, fetching water from the nearby stream and boiling it on the Littlewoods stove within the cabin. This doctor adhered to the relatively new practice of sterilising cutting instruments, a sign of progress in their medical approach.

Initially, the boss resisted the notion of losing consciousness while someone wielded sharp instruments over him. However, the doctor persisted. With the boss still awake, the doctor began probing for the bullet. The pain, excruciating due to the bullet's depth, swiftly convinced the boss of the necessity for an anaesthetic. The doctor soaked a cloth with ether and placed it over the boss's mouth and nose. Within seconds, the boss succumbed, going limp. Now, unencumbered by the wounded man's movements, the doctor could probe for the bullet without hindrance.

The room held its breath; the tension was palpable as the doctor worked to extract the embedded projectile. The doctor meticulously tended to the boss's unconscious form for over half an hour. After fifteen intense minutes, the doctor finally extracted the bullet. Holding up the bloody, misshapen piece of lead, the doctor examined it before dropping it into a tin dishpan, where it landed with a resounding clunk.

Despite the successful removal of the bullet, the doctor deemed it necessary to excise some of the surrounding flesh—time had allowed the wound to begin mortifying. Addressing the onlookers, the doctor emphasised the importance of preventing gangrene: "We don't want to save him from the bullet only to lose him to infection."

With that, the doctor turned his attention to Byron. Examining his wound, the doctor nodded approvingly. "You've been diligent," he remarked. "Nice and clean, no signs of infection."

The doctor applied salve to the raw flesh, eliciting a stinging sensation. Drawing on his wound experience, Byron felt optimistic—he knew he'd recover within a few days.

The doctor straightened up and inquired, "Now, can I go home?"

Boulder Ross scoffed, "Don't be foolish, Doctor. We can't release you until we're ready to depart ourselves."

"And frankly, I don't envision him"—he gestured towards the unconscious boss—"mounting a horse anytime soon."

The doctor conceded, "No." He predicted, "He'll remain quite ill for at least a week. Once he's on the mend, then you can go home. Understood?"

The doctor nodded woodenly, acknowledging the situation.

After the bullet extraction, the boss remained unconscious for the first two days. Occasionally, he would rouse himself to inquire about Ross and Phillips' progress and whether any signs of pursuit loomed. Initially, there were none.

However, Ross's excursion to replenish their dwindling food supplies altered the landscape. Upon his return to the cabin, Ross appeared agitated, sweat-soaked, and distressed. He confided to Phillips in hushed tones, "God, the entire damn expanse down in the flats is teeming with posses and lawmen. I think they're scouring the area, possibly searching for us."

The situation had escalated, and the stakes were higher than ever. The tension hung thick in the air.

The situation revolves around a group of people in a tight spot. They suspect the doctor they encountered earlier might have raised an alarm about their presence. Now, they urgently need to escape. One suggested prioritising their safety over the injured boss, who was still recovering in the nearby cabin. The boss owes them a significant amount of money, and they believe they can live comfortably if they reach Mexico. However, the boss will likely part with that money if they willingly escape. Moreover, their hideout, well-concealed in a secluded box canyon, makes it difficult for anyone to find them—unless they know the exact location. Ross, one of the group members, points out that staying quiet and hidden is their best chance of avoiding detection. Byron, another member, is acutely aware of the risks they face. In summary, their escape plan depends on evading capture, relying on their knowledge of the hidden location, and prioritising their survival over the boss's well-being. The tension and urgency are palpable as they weigh their options and consider the consequences.

Byron's senses sharpened as he sat in the sun outside the cabin. Nearby, Greg watched the doctor, who diligently tended bandages by the stream. Meanwhile, Ross and Phillips huddled inside, conferring with the boss, whose health had remarkably improved.

Byron's intuition kicked in. The doctor had drawn everyone's attention, creating an opportunity. Silently, he circumvented the cabin, skirting along the back wall toward the sole window. Once glazed, it now harboured only grimy shards at its base—a portal into the cabin. With their survival in jeopardy, Byron strained to comprehend every word that passed within those walls. The urgency hung heavy as the boss's voice sliced through the tension.

"The doctor must go," he declared, his tone as icy and authoritative as ever, even in his weakened state.

The doctor had glimpsed Byron's face, and uncertainty gnawed at them. Could the doctor recognise him? The stakes were high; exposure would be disastrous. Inside the cabin, Dean Phillips shifted restlessly. His voice, sharp and decisive, cut through the room.

"I'll handle it now," he offered, ready to eliminate the threat.

But the boss held them back. "Not yet," he countered. "We can't act until we're certain we've extracted all we need from him."

The delicate balance between survival and betrayal teetered, and Byron knew they were walking a treacherous path. The boss's voice broke the silence. "Okay, it can wait," he conceded. But then he continued, hinting at another matter that demanded attention. Byron, the focus of his words, listened intently. Despite lacking concrete evidence, the boss harboured suspicions about their newest member—the doctor. Trouble seemed to follow him like a shadow. The recent bank heist, swarming with unexpected adversaries, felt too orchestrated to be a coincidence. Someone had betrayed them.

The boss's gaze shifted to Boulder Ross, a fellow conspirator. How had Ross infiltrated their ranks? The boss had kept a vigilant eye on him, yet somehow Ross had slipped past their defences. The truth remained elusive, but one thing was clear: their survival depended on unravelling the mystery. And only Byron held the key—the secret destination known only to him. The tension thickened, and Byron grappled with the weight of their shared fate.

The tension in the cabin was palpable as the boss's suspicions about Byron escalated. Ross had unwittingly become a focal point of danger. The boss's voice cut through the air, revealing unsettling truths. "Yes," the boss confirmed, "there's a wanted poster for him, you say, Ross. The U.S. Marshals are offering a five-hundred-dollar reward for his capture." The revelation hung heavy, casting shadows on their already precarious situation.

Ross, agitated, blurted out, "Is he one of them? A marshal?"

The boss's icy response pierced the room. "It's entirely possible," he said. "But let's consider the consequences. Since Ross joined us, chaos has ensued. Our survival hinges on unravelling this mystery."

Ross's anger flared. "I'll kill him right now!"

But the boss intervened. "Hold on, Ross. Byron, the doctor, is no ordinary man. He's dangerous. Shooting him would attract unwanted attention. If other people are hunting in this area, gunfire would lead them straight to us." Their options narrowed, and the cabin walls seemed to close in as they grappled with the weight of their choices.

"Wait!" The boss's voice cut through the tension. Ross's agreement was filled with anger. "Okay," he grumbled.

"Now," the boss continued, "go outside and fetch Greg. I need to speak with him."

Ross echoed incredulously, "That guy's been griping nonstop about our measly bank haul, but he won't be complaining after our little chat."

Byron listened as the boots shuffled away. "Greg!" Ross's voice carried. "Get your ass in here. The boss wants a word." The air thickened with anticipation. Byron remained pressed against the cabin's rear wall. Ross and Phillips loitered outside, increasing the risk of discovery. Yet curiosity drove him. What secrets would the boss share with Greg—the shiftless, dim-witted crew member? It seemed like an unlikely confidant.

However, Byron didn't have much to lose, as he was already in a precarious situation. If they found him eavesdropping, the inevitable confrontation would occur sooner. Strangely, he almost welcomed it. Yet his most significant concern lay elsewhere: the doctor. Without assistance, the doctor's chances of survival dwindled. Byron resolved to ensure the doctor's escape. These were no ordinary killers—the coldest, most ruthless he'd encountered.

Greg's heavy footsteps echoed as he entered the cabin. "You wanted to see me, boss?" he inquired.

"Yes, Greg." The boss's voice cut through the air, businesslike and urgent. "I need your assistance on a critical mission."

"Me?" Greg's surprise was evident.

The boss leaned in. "Listen carefully. I need you to deliver a message—to my wife. She believes I'm away on a brief business trip. But she might panic and report me missing if I don't return soon. We can't afford that scrutiny, especially after the recent robberies. Understand?"

Greg hesitated. "So, you want me to reassure her? Let her know you're okay?"

The boss's patience waned. "I'll handle that part. You'll take her a private note. No witnesses. Just deliver it discreetly. And remember, there's more to that note than meets the eye."

Greg's sullen agreement hung in the air. The stakes were high, and secrets simmered beneath the surface.

"Ah-ah, what?" Greg's voice wavered, a hint of nervousness creeping in. But then the boss dropped a bombshell: "Ten thousand dollars."

Greg's disbelief was palpable. The boss leaned in, revealing the covert plan. "Listen carefully," he said. "The note will instruct my wife to send a bank draft—a sight draft—to a specific bank under a certain name. When we retrieve that money, Greg, you, I, and others will share it. Ten thousand dollars will be yours."

Greg couldn't contain himself. "Goddamn!" he burst out. The promise of such wealth left him reeling—ten thousand dollars, a fortune that could change everything. The boss's calm demeanour masked the high stakes, but Greg understood this was no ordinary mission. And for that kind of money, he'd better tread carefully.

"Right," the boss instructed, handing Greg the note. "Make sure my wife receives this. I've already written it. Can you read, Greg?"

Greg's affirmative response was hesitant but sufficient. Greg inscribed his name and address on the front of the note. Byron strained to catch Greg's mumbled words as he deciphered the address.

"Cheyenne, huh?" Greg finally remarked.

"Yes," the boss confirmed. "Now, move swiftly. It'll take two days to ride there and another two to return. No dawdling. Be back here in four days. By then, I should be fit enough to ride. We'll collect your ten thousand dollars."

"Understood, boss," Greg replied, his excitement palpable. He hurried out of the cabin, visions of sudden wealth dancing in his mind. Meanwhile, Byron sensed no further revelations awaited him; he slipped away quietly, tracing a wide arc so that he approached from the opposite direction when the cabin came into view again. Greg was already saddling up, his determination unwavering. The allure of those ten thousand dollars had ultimately captured him. Byron grappled with the weight of his knowledge—his dangerous secrets. If his mission succeeded, he'd be the sole bearer of the boss's true identity.

Shrouded in mystery, the boss seemed like a man of influence who wouldn't tolerate any loose ends connecting him to the recent spree of robberies. Greg, however, lacked such foresight. His reward for delivering the note would likely be a bullet in the back. But logic wasn't Greg's strong suit; that's probably why the boss had chosen him. Once he regained his strength, the boss's intentions became chillingly clear: a wholesale slaughter awaited, marking Byron, the doctor, and Greg for death.

Now, Byron faced a critical decision. Should he strike pre-emptively, confronting them before they could ambush him? Leaving wasn't an option; abandoning the doctor to their mercy was unthinkable. And the gnawing curiosity about the boss's true identity kept him tethered—a mystery he couldn't leave unsolved. Byron found himself in a precarious situation. The horses were conveniently stabled right next to the cabin; their presence was impossible to ignore. Escape would be futile without a horse; the boss would track him down within miles. Perhaps the boss's suspicions would wane, and they wouldn't turn on him. But could he count on that?

For the next three days, Byron played the role of ignorance, avoiding any hint of their plans or suspicions. But the fourth day loomed—the day Greg was due to return. Now well enough to venture outside, the boss basked in the sun. Despite lingering weakness and pain, he exuded determination. The doctor marvelled at the rapid recovery, blissfully unaware that the moment the wounded man could ride, Byron's life would hang by a thread.

And then, on that fateful morning, Byron's opportunity arrived. Boulder Ross, who had once guarded the doctor, grew restless.

"Byron," Ross instructed, "take over for me. I've got matters to attend to."

The stakes were high, and Byron knew he had to act swiftly. Ross was likely to find a hidden bottle somewhere. The boss slept inside the cabin as Ross vanished up the box canyon. Dean Phillips lingered by the stream, absentmindedly tossing pebbles. Now, along with the doctor, Byron leaned in.

"This is our chance, doc," he murmured.

The doctor, disconsolate on a rock, snapped to attention. Suspicion etched his features. "What are you talking about?"

Byron's voice dropped even lower. "Time to escape," he declared.

The doctor's confusion was evident. "You don't seriously believe they'll spare your life, do you?" Byron prodded.

The doctor hesitated and then asked, "Why are you...?"

"I'm not one of them," Byron interrupted. "I'm a U.S. marshal, undercover. My mission was to dismantle this gang, but things went sideways. They're onto me now. It's time to slip away, both of us."

The doctor grappled with the revelation. "But they'll kill me?"

"Yup," Byron confirmed. "I overheard their plans. Now, are you ready to make a run for it?"

The doctor's decision came swiftly. "I guess I have no choice. But how do we reach the horses? Going around the cabin would expose us."

"We'll go without horses," Byron asserted. "We'll go on foot. We'll find a horse down the trail. Stop asking questions and come with me."

The doctor hesitated, then resolved, "I'm with you."

"Good," Byron whispered. "Let's go."

Their escape hung in the balance, and the cabin's walls seemed to close in, urging them onward. Byron and the doctor moved swiftly, leaving the cabin's vicinity. Their escape route led them out of Little Box Canyon within 15 minutes. This initial part of their escape posed the most significant danger—if they were missed too soon, they'd be easily found. But as they ventured further away, their chances of avoiding detection improved. Luck seemed to favour them. For half an hour, they walked without any signs of pursuit. Now, well beyond the box canyon, they followed a faint trail.

Suddenly, Byron's senses sharpened. He heard a distant horseman's approach.

"Get off the path," Byron whispered to the doctor. "Hide in the brush."

"But what about you?" the doctor demanded.

"Shut up and move," Byron snarled.

The doctor bustled into the underbrush while Byron positioned himself closer to the trail. Moments later, Greg rode into view on a weary horse. Byron stepped out into the open.

"Jesus!" Greg exclaimed, reaching for his gun. "Byron, what the hell are you doing here? Are you walking?"

Greg was intrigued by Byron's sluggish response. "That's an interesting story," he drawled.

"What the hell are you talking about?" Greg pressed.

Byron's smile held a hint of menace. "You didn't think they'd let you live?"

Byron stared at Greg, his eyes hard and calculating. "Use your brains if you've got any," he retorted. "You're the only man alive who knows who the boss is and where he lives. The boss can't afford to let any of us know that. Do you believe he will allow you to live despite the possibility that you will become inebriated and vomit at some point?"

Greg's confusion was evident. "How did you know I went to see the boss's wife?"

"He told me," Byron replied coolly. "He lured you down here and set you up. And that ten thousand dollars? He laughed when he said you'd believe he'd give it to you."

Greg's jaw hung open. Byron's words struck him as true. How else could Byron have known about Greg's whereabouts unless the boss had spilt the beans? The realisation hit Greg like a punch.

"You came here to bushwhack me?" Greg demanded, his hand inching towards his revolver.

Byron's smirk remained. "Relax. Had I intended to bushwhack you, I would have already done so; I wouldn't be standing here having this conversation."

"Well then, what the hell?" His voice trailed off, the gravity of the situation sinking in.

Byron's voice dripped with disgust as he spoke, "I don't ambush men I've ridden with. I merely faked it because I knew my survival depended on it. We must decide, buddy: either escape from here or confront those treacherous backstabbers head-on."

"Yeah, you're right," Greg agreed. "Damn it all! I was already counting on that ten thousand bucks. But where's your horse?"

"I couldn't get it away from the cabin. It looks like we'll have to ride double."

"Double up?" Byron scoffed. "Even with the best horses in the world, we'd be lucky to survive these mountains. The law is closing in, searching everywhere. And to think, I risked my life by riding back here to warn that treacherous individual. A big-shot banker, no less."

Greg raised an eyebrow. "A banker, you say? Well, that's rich. It turns out he's been robbing banks while working for one of Cheyenne's largest financial institutions. James Van de Velt, as they call him. A real fancy name to match his real fancy job."

His eyes widened as he surveyed the trail ahead. "And look there! Jesus, he's coming this way, flanked by Ross and Phillips." Byron's mind raced as the pursuit closed in. The men from the cabin had tracked him and the doctor relentlessly. With his face twisted in anger, Greg yanked his rifle from its sheath above. A split second later, a shot echoed down the trail, with the bullet slamming into Greg almost simultaneously. A second bullet hit Greg, causing him to grunt, slump in the saddle, and manage to return fire. This time, the slug knocked him off the rear of his horse, his rifle tumbling to the ground not far from Byron.

Byron seized the weapon, stealing a glance at Greg's lifeless form. The man looked as dead as anyone could be. Without hesitation, Byron sprinted into the brush, following the general direction where the doctor had vanished. "Doc! Where the hell are you?" he called out desperately. The voice came from behind a thicket, and Byron discovered the doctor crouched there. The sparse cover offered little protection; standing up would be suicidal.

"Hoof beats," reverberated from the trail. "Greg's dead," someone's voice announced. "Now, where the hell are Byron and Doc?" Phillips stepped in. "I see tracks leading into the brush. Let's go in and get them." But the boss intervened. "No," he said. "Let's ride up the trail and gain some height. Then, we can pick them off at will. Hell, why don't we ride on out?"

Ross's voice chimed in. "We can't leave them alive. Greg may have spilt something on Byron before we got him." Byron clenched his jaw. "Well, hell," he muttered. "Let's get it over with, then." The sound of hoof beats faded as they rode away up the trail. Byron turned to the doctor, holding up the rifle. "Can you shoot?" he asked urgently.

The doctor's urgent voice pierced the chaos. "Over there. I found some rocks." Byron sprinted towards the sound, bullets zipping past him. As he reached the small cluster of boulders, he realized the doctor had been right—a precarious refuge awaited them. Already, the doctor huddled behind the rocks, firing towards the skyline. Byron took cover and assessed their new position. The boulders formed a rough line, their faces tilted upward. For the moment, they offered a modicum of safety. But that respite would be fleeting.

From above, the boss's calm voice issued orders. "Phillips, flank them from the right. Ross, take the left." Byron clenched his teeth. The boulders' alignment meant they provided cover in only one direction. Once Ross and Phillips positioned themselves on either side, he and the doctor would be easy prey. He fired shots at Ross, who was manoeuvring around the side. Meanwhile, the doctor kept Phillips at bay. The firing tapered off.

Nobody had any real targets yet, so everyone was saving ammunition.

While Byron was desperately looking around for better cover in this lull, he thought he heard a distant shout from down below them. He had just about dismissed it as a figment of his imagination when Boulder Ross called out from above. "Goddamn, boss! There's a whole bunch of riders heading up this way!" A long stream of curses came from the boss. "A posse!" he shouted. "They must have heard the shooting. Come on, boys, we've got to finish off Byron."

Dissent arose among the men. "You finish him off. I'm hauling ass," one of them protested. "Me too!" another voice chimed in, panic evident. The boss unleashed a torrent of curses and fired several desperate shots at Byron before disappearing himself. A few moments later, Byron heard the sound of horses galloping up the trail.

Byron stood up and raced towards the trail, the doctor close behind him. From below, he could hear shouts and the sound of riders approaching. Greg's horse was still standing on the trail near its late master's body, probably too tired to run. Byron climbed into the saddle, the horse giving a grunt of resignation.

A group of horsemen came pounding into sight a minute later, led by a big man on a grey horse. The riders were all armed, rifles raised to cover Byron. "No. Hold your fire," the big man ordered, waving gun muzzles down. "He's one of ours." He pulled his horse up next to Byron's mount. "You are still one of ours, aren't you, Byron?" he asked, grinning. "We were wondering... the way you keep riding off with those bandits."

"Hello, Stephen. I'm still one of yours, but three of them are getting away over the hill. Let's go after them. Just leave a couple of men here to take care of the doctor."

The doctor insisted on riding along, doubled behind one of the marshals. "I intend to manufacture a gunshot patient out of one of those bastards!" he snarled. "Kidnapping me, planning to kill me... they better ride hard and fast."

Unfortunately, the posse's horses and Greg's mount were tired from the long haul up from below. Nevertheless, the marshals pushed on and, in another few minutes, came to the entrance of the little box canyon. Byron urged the others to slow down, warning that they may try to bushwhack them. But they reached the cabin without incident.

Upon entering, it was evident that the fugitives had quickly removed most of their belongings from the cabin. Tracks led further up into the canyon. Byron knew there was no way out in that direction, but he cursed himself for not making sure earlier. "Come on; let's go after them, Stephen." The posse continued up the canyon, its walls beginning to narrow, rising steeply on either side. It was imperative to ride carefully, be alert for a desperate last-ditch stand by the fugitives.

"I think we got them, Byron," Stephen said excitedly. "There isn't any way out." Byron and Stephen, their nerves taut as bowstrings, surveyed the treacherous terrain. The narrow aperture yawned before them—a passage so tight that riders would have to thread through it in a single file. The sheer cliffs on either side seemed to mock their progress, rising like ancient sentinels guarding Stephen's unease.

"I sure as hell don't like the looks of that," he muttered, his eyes tracing the jagged edges of the rocky walls. Byron nodded in agreement. They knew they had no choice but to proceed cautiously, with every sense alert and fingers poised near their holstered guns.

Byron's ears pricked up as the posse inched forward, the first rider nearing the cleft's entrance. A faint hissing sound reached him, barely audible over the wind's whisper. He looked up, his heart pounding. The precipices above were a mosaic of fractured rock and loose earth, a precarious balance of nature's fury. Then he saw a plume of grey smoke, spitting sparks like an angry serpent. The canyon was no mere passage; it was a trap. The outlaws had rigged it, waiting for unsuspecting pursuers.

Byron's instincts screamed at him. "Back!" he shouted, wheeling his horse. "Get the hell back down the canyon!" The posse scattered, retreating from the deadly funnel. The aperture, once a potential escape route, now held only menace. As the smoke billowed, Byron wondered how many lives hung in the balance. The chase had taken them to the brink, and survival demanded a desperate retreat.

Byron vowed to outwit their cunning foes in that narrow gorge, where shadows clung like vengeful ghosts. The canyon would not claim them today. Not if he could help it. And so, with adrenaline coursing through his veins, he spurred his horse, urging it away from danger. Behind him, Stephen followed, eyes wide and hearts racing. The hunt had turned, and the hunted had become the prey. But Byron would fight. For justice, for redemption, and for the promise of another dawn.

"You bastard, you got away with it once more," he murmured. "However, the game will be different this time, as I am now aware of your name, Mr. Daniel van de Velt."

9

THE VAN DE VELT HOUSE

Van de Velt, Ross, and Phillips had vanished up the dynamite cleft, leaving Byron and the doctor to descend the mountain with Stephen and the rest of the Marshalls. After dropping off the doctor, Stephen and Byron wasted no time. They wired the United States Marshal's agency in Virginia, reporting their findings. Their journey continued, riding hard towards Cheyenne. They changed horses twice along the way, arriving in the bustling town by early afternoon the next day.

Their first order of business was an inquiry at the local bank regarding Mr Daniel Van de Velt. The bank officers initially guarded their responses, eyeing the dusty, sweat-streaked duo warily. However, fate intervened. Mr James Christopher Gardiner, the highly regarded head of the United States Marshals' Western regional office, had traversed the plugged trails, chasing down the nation's most hardened desperadoes, much like Byron was doing now. His reputation for bravery and fair dealings preceded him, earning him respect throughout the West. Few others could silence Byron, but Gardiner was one of them.

"Mr James," Mr James Christopher Gardiner addressed the bank president in a conciliatory tone, saying, "I understand your concern. Perhaps there's been an error, but charges have been levelled, and the best course of action is a thorough investigation. If you could kindly provide us with Mr Larraine Van de Velt's address..." The steel beneath Gardiner's smooth words was palpable. Mr Logan, the bank president, complied, revealing the crucial information that led them to the house. Gardiner was well-known and highly respected throughout the West.

The Van de Velt House: A Tale of Intrigue and Unwanted Visitors

In the heart of the town, nestled amidst sprawling grounds, stood the Van de Velt House, an imposing residence that commanded attention. Its grandeur was evident: a large, expensive abode meticulously positioned in the most coveted part of town. The property boasted not only the main house but also several intriguing features. A separate servant's house stood to the rear and one side of the main house—a testament to the family's affluence. These structures added character to the estate, depicting a life of privilege and leisure.

The landscape was equally enchanting. Trees cast dappled shadows on the manicured lawns below. Flowerbeds burst forth with vibrant colours, creating a picturesque scene. It was unmistakably the residence of a prominent banker, Mr Daniel Van de Velt. Yet, despite the luxury, an air of discomfort lingered. Byron, standing on the porch, felt it keenly. It was not the house that unsettled him; instead, it was the company he found himself in—an assembly of unwelcome guests. The Van de Velt House held secrets, and its occupants were about to face scrutiny like never before.

Daniel Van de Velt's wife stood uncertainly in the doorway, her confusion evident.

"You," she hesitated, "you want to come into our house? You want to search through Daniel's belongings?" Her eyes darted between the imposing figures on her front porch.

"Yes, ma'am," the local sheriff replied, his discomfort apparent. "We have a warrant. I'm afraid you'll have to let us in, Mrs Van de Velt."

"But I..." Mrs Lorraine Van de Velt hesitated, her eyes darting between the imposing men who had just entered her home.

The Van de Velt House's interior surpassed even its impressive exterior. Rich hardwood panels adorned the walls, each piece a testament to refined taste. Works of art graced the panels, their colours and forms capturing attention. The house spoke of wealth—a little better appointed than a bank vice president's usual abode.

"Must you go up there?" Mrs Van de Velt's voice trembled. She watched as Byron and Gardiner disappeared from view, their purpose clear. Meanwhile, the sheriff and a deputy explored the parlour and living room, unravelling the mysteries concealed within these lavish walls.

As Byron and Gardiner ascended the grand staircase to the second floor, they marvelled at the luxury. The hardwood floors were covered with exquisite carpets, their intricate patterns hinting at distant lands and adventures. In the dining area, silver cutlery gleamed alongside delicate china housed within elegant cupboards. The upstairs consisted of several bedrooms, a library, and a study.

"In here!" Byron called out.

Gardiner entered the room and looked where Byron was pointing.

"That is him," Byron said. "That is the boss."

They met Mrs Van de Velt downstairs, her anxiety palpable as she clutched the edge of a chair in the living room. Gardiner, holding up the photograph, addressed her sternly.

"Can you tell me who this is, ma'am?"

"Why, what are you doing with that?" Her voice was sharp, her eyes narrowing. "You have no right."

"I'm afraid we do, ma'am," Gardiner interrupted. "Now, if you could just tell me…"

The anger in her voice was unmistakable. "It's my husband, of course," she snapped. "I don't like you. What are you doing?"

Gardiner ignored her remarks and manipulated the back of the frame.

"I'm sorry, ma'am," he said, his demeanour seemingly genuine. But his next move revealed a different purpose. He beckoned over the man from the Virginia office, extracting the photograph from its frame and handing it to him.

"Take this and find a photographer," Gardiner instructed. "Make copies. Ensure one reaches the kidnapped doctor; let him confirm identification. And don't forget our rogues' gallery. Oh, and prepare a wanted poster, of course."

Mrs Van de Velt's face contorted in incredulous horror.

"You... you can't be serious," she burst out. "You'll regret everything you've done. My husband holds considerable standing and importance in Cheyenne. When he returns and discovers your actions—"

The Van de Velt House buzzed with tension as small children burst into the living room, their voices echoing off the opulent walls. A nursemaid trailed behind them, her uniform dishevelled.

"Mummy! Mummy!" one of the little girls cried out. "There are a lot of men in the other room. They're taking things."

The children fell silent as they caught sight of Byron, Gardiner, and the other U.S. Marshals operatives. Mrs Van de Velt gathered the girls close.

"See? See what you're doing?" she pleaded. "You're upsetting Freya and Amelie."

Tears welled in her eyes, and Byron averted his gaze. He despised this part of the job—the intrusion into a family's life, the shattering of illusions. He would rather face down the notorious trio—boss, Dean Phillips, and Boulder Ross—all three of them, guns drawn, than be here now, dismantling this woman's world.

The sheriff entered, holding out a slip of paper.

"Is this what you were talking about?" he asked, handing it to Byron.

The receipt revealed a telegraph bank draft for twenty thousand dollars from Mrs Van de Velt, care of Daniel Van de Velt's bank, to a confident Bob Mitchell, care of a distant bank. It clicked into place—the money the boss had sent Greg for. The puzzle was coming together, but the cost weighed heavily on Byron's conscience.

In the quiet town of Elmwood, where secrets whispered through cobblestone streets, Daniel Van de Velt stood as a figure of unwavering respect. His multifaceted role in the community painted a portrait of influence: not only was he the esteemed bank officer, but he was also a devoted deacon in the local church, an active member of civic groups, and a generous supporter of charitable causes. Yet, beneath the veneer of admiration, dissenting voices lingered. These were the murmurs of men who bore scars from their encounters with Van de Velt—a man whose cruelty cut more deeply than the sharpest blade.

Initially dismissed as jealousy from business rivals, these dissenters soon revealed a pattern. As investigators delved into Van de Velt's financial affairs, a modus operandi emerged. The bank he presided over had murky connections—threads that wove through the very fabric of the town. Mines, other banks, corporate offices, and even individual lives intersected with Van de Velt's institution. The question remained: Was he a guardian of prosperity or a puppet master pulling strings in the shadows?

As the investigation continued, the once-obscure banker revealed layers of complexity. Like the town itself, his life held secrets waiting to be unravelled. And in the heart of Newton, where allegiances blurred and allegories unfolded, Daniel Van de Velt remained an enigma—an intricate puzzle with missing pieces yet to be found.

Byron's hushed revelation echoed through the dimly lit room. The pieces fell into place as he pored over Daniel Van de Velt's meticulously kept banking records. The boss's uncanny familiarity with the mine's intricate machinery and the bank's labyrinthine transactions was no coincidence. Van de Velt's knowledge transcended mere numbers. He intimately understood the mine's veins—where wealth flowed like lifeblood—and the bank's vaults, where fortunes lay dormant.

However, it didn't stop there. His insights reached deeper, infiltrating the very sinews of the organisations themselves—their vulnerabilities, hidden alliances, and Achilles' heels. Trust had been Van de Velt's currency. As a respected figure in town, he moved seamlessly between worlds—the polished bank officer, the devout deacon, and the civic leader. His position afforded him access to the inner sanctums of power, where secrets were whispered and deals were struck. And in those clandestine exchanges, he

harvested the seeds of success.

Raids—the daring heists that left the town both amazed and terrified—were choreographed with surgical precision. Van de Velt's raids were not blind gambles but calculated manoeuvres. He knew which strings to pull, which doors to unlock, and which guards to distract. His raids bore the mark of a man who had studied his prey—their habits, weaknesses, and darkest desires.

Byron leaned closer to the ledger, tracing the inked trails of Van de Velt's exploits. The man was no mere outlaw; he was a maestro orchestrating a symphony of chaos. And as the town grappled with its conflicting narratives—the benevolent benefactor versus the cunning puppeteer—one truth emerged: Daniel Van de Velt was a master of shadows, weaving his legacy in ink and intrigue.

The tenacious investigator Byron stumbled upon a dissonant chord in Daniel Van de Velt's otherwise harmonious reputation. While Gardiner and the rest of the team meticulously traced the threads of Van de Velt's banking connections, Byron delved into the shadowed underbelly of Cheyenne—the murky alleys, the dimly lit saloons, and the brothels discreetly tucked away from the town hall. His motivation was personal. Having encountered Van de Velt on the trail, Byron glimpsed beyond the facade—the veneer of social respectability that most townspeople admired. Another side to the man existed, a hidden chamber where darkness thrived. And in these dimly lit corners, Byron, the persistent investigator, uncovered a conflicting element in Daniel Van de Velt's generally consistent reputation.

Gardiner and the other crewmembers diligently followed the paths of Van de Velt's financial associations, while Byron delved into the concealed and questionable aspects of Cheyenne, such as the obscure alleyways, dimly lit taverns, and discreetly located brothels, hidden from public view. His motivation was purely personal. Upon encountering Van de Velt on his journey, Byron gained insight into the true nature lying beneath the surface— the superficial appearance of social acceptability that most locals adored. The man's hidden room, where darkness thrived, symbolised his other ego.

Byron saw a real embodiment of Van de Velt's duality in these poorly lit areas: a woman who practised her profession in a dilapidated bar at the town's outskirts, maintaining a captivating attractiveness despite the hardships of life. She expressed contempt, her lips forming a mocking smirk, as she said, "Daniel Van de Velt? I have a thorough knowledge of him. That was a really distressing experience. He always compensated me well." Her gaze appeared unfocused, and her speech gradually diminished, as though memories were etched into the creases of her countenance. "However, there were actions that he performed—actions that I would prefer to erase from my memory."

A clandestine and ruthless group was masterminding audacious heists and brutal homicides, while the town's rumours created an atmosphere of fear and apprehension. Daniel Van de Velt, a person whose fundamental nature seemed forged in darkness, was at the focal point of those accusations. The tales were confirmed by the exhausted woman, whose eyes bore the burden of her profession.

"Indeed, there was something distinctly unusual about that person."

Byron leaned in to uncover the truth. "Where is he most likely to be located?"

The woman's laughter lacked enjoyment. "I was not his drinking companion," she declared, avoiding eye contact.

Consequently, the enigma grew more intricate. Daniel Van de Velt, the ruthless manipulator and esteemed individual, remained difficult to find. The town was divided between deep respect and intense fear as his dual life balanced on the boundary of ethical principles. Byron made a firm decision to reveal the truth as the darkness became stronger. Perhaps this truth was hidden beneath the woman's tired appearance. Byron's focus was captivated by her words as she spoke.

A perplexing phenomenon that resisted easy classification was found within Van de Velt. Reports of a criminal syndicate implicated in audacious heists and ruthless homicides were spreading across the community. The town's whispers had woven a tapestry of dread—a gang, elusive and merciless, orchestrating daring robberies and brutal killings. And at the heart of those rumours stood Daniel Van de Velt, a man whose very essence seemed forged in shadows. The weary woman confirmed the tales.

Byron believed it all, with a gut feeling sharper than any blade. Daniel Van de Velt, the respected figure, harboured a darker calling that danced on the edge of morality. As the investigation deepened, Byron grappled with the truth. If there existed a man tailor-made for violence and cunning, it was the very embodiment of Elmwood's contradictions: good old Daniel Van de Velt. He was a master of shadows, a conductor of chaos, and perhaps the key to unravelling the town's intricate web of secrets.

Following her husband's instructions, Mrs Van de Velt's bank draft had been meticulously traced. Alas, it had already been cashed several days prior. The recipient aligned with Daniel Van de Velt's description, but he vanished once the currency exchanged hands, a phantom slipping through the town's grasp.

Gardiner, his expression etched with frustration, voiced the inevitable truth. "A man like him," he lamented, "is likely en route to Europe or South America by now." The ports and shipping lines had been alerted, and Van de Velt's visage broadcast everywhere. Yet silence echoed back into a void where answers should have bloomed. Perhaps he had already fled the country, or maybe he lay low, waiting for the collective memory to fade.

Byron interjected, scepticism in his tone. "Hard to believe he'd take Ross and Phillips with him—the other two gang members, partners in crime, bound by blood and shared secrets."

"Who knows?" Byron mused. "He wields wealth like a blade. His financial affairs reveal a subtle imbalance—a surplus beyond salary and investments, but that surplus doesn't account for the gang's entire haul." Van de Velt, the elusive puppeteer, had squirreled away fortunes hidden in caches, perhaps safeguarding his life. His banking acumen was a double-edged sword—the knowledge that could unravel him also shielded his secrets.

Therefore, the hunt continued—a relentless pursuit through shadows and whispers, chasing a man who danced on the precipice of revelation. Byron concurred silently. Daniel Van de Velt was a formidable adversary, with his intricate knowledge of banking intricacies. Catching him would be akin to chasing shadows—a relentless pursuit through labyrinthine alleys and hidden vaults.

However, Byron harboured doubts about his involvement in the chase. Did he genuinely want to be part of this dangerous game? Then, on the third day of his stay in Cheyenne, the sheriff arrived with grim tidings. Gardiner, holed up in the downtown hotel, joined Byron for their afternoon conference. The sheriff's breathless entrance disrupted their deliberations.

"It's Mrs Lorraine Van de Velt," he exclaimed. "She's had some kind of breakdown." The words hung heavy in the room. "Tried to take her own life and that of the children—poisoning them—ghastly. The nursemaid saved them, but the doctors believe she is beyond recovery. An institution might be her only refuge."

Byron turned away, his disgust palpable. "Son of a bitch!" he muttered under his breath. "Goddamn, Daniel Van de Velt!"

The man's banditry had not only robbed banks but had also stolen something far more precious: a good woman's sanity. Lorraine, gentle and well-educated, now teetered on the edge of oblivion. Van de Velt's twisted benevolence—whatever drove him to a life of needless crime—had wielded a pistol more lethal than any firearm. This weapon sparked despair and shattered lives.

Gardiner scrutinised Byron, recognising him as perhaps the finest operative—especially when facing down hardened desperados in gritty showdowns. But this delicate inquiry wasn't Byron's forte.

"How are you holding up?" Gardiner asked abruptly, his gaze probing.

Byron's mind shifted to the wound he had acquired during the bank robbery. "Oh, fine. A little sore now and then."

Gardiner leaned in, concern etching his features. "Look, why don't you take a month off? Rest up."

Byron considered the suggestion. "Not a bad idea."

However, Gardiner, who knew Byron best, issued a warning. "Bullshit. You'll be off chasing that girl. What's her name? Abigail?"

Byron's cheeks reddened. "Yeah, Abigail."

"Remember," Gardiner warned, "don't go running off and getting married like your scallywag partner, Doc. We need you."

Byron's gaze locked with Gardiner's. "I cannot make any promises," he growled, then turned and strode out of the hotel.

Gardiner muttered to himself, frustration simmering. "Oh, goddammit. Don't tell me I'm going to lose another good man."

10

A JOURNEY TO ABIGAIL'S HOUSE

Byron embarked on a journey to Abigail's house the following day. Abigail resided in the mid-eastern region of Kansas, about two days' ride west of the city, making the trip lengthy. Although he could have traveled by rail, which would have significantly shortened the journey, Byron chose to ride horseback instead. He felt the need for solitude and contemplation during the ride. Along the way, he deliberately avoided towns, spending nights outdoors, often with his horse reins securely in hand. The terrain was rugged and challenging.

During his journey, Byron noticed a small group of Indians, four of whom were perched on horseback atop a distant hill. They watched him closely from about a mile away. Byron quickly mounted his horse and rode in the opposite direction. Occasionally, he encountered other travelers passing through the area from the

Dakotas and Colorado. However, this particular band of Indians didn't trouble him; they were likely young men seeking horses to steal. Byron remained relatively unconcerned, knowing that such a small group of Indians would not attack a well-armed white man like himself.

As Byron traveled through northern Kansas, approaching the Arkansas River, he felt someone following him. Initially, he could not discern who it was; he merely caught glimpses of movement behind him. Eventually, he halted in a thicket, retrieving his binoculars to scrutinize the trail behind him. Emerging from a shallow depression, the men revealed themselves, their gaze fixed on the ground as they doggedly tracked his every move. Byron understood that these white outlaws posed a more significant threat than the Indians did. These ruthless men would rob and kill travelers for a mere pittance, sometimes just a few dollars. Byron's horse and weapons were valuable assets, but the three hundred dollars he carried in his pockets were even more precious.

Through the binoculars, Byron studied the men until their faces became distinct. It was the Mitchell brothers and one other, a trio notorious for their violent exploits. Their images had graced the agency's most-wanted gallery for nearly a year, a consequence of their prolonged spree of murder, rape, and robbery. That evening, Byron cleaned his campsite with extra care, making it look as if he were being careless. He built a big fire in a bit of depression surrounded by heavy brush, stuffed his bedroll with a brush to make it look like someone was sleeping in it, and tied his horse tightly to a sturdy tree about twenty yards away.

As the fire died down, Byron stepped back into the brush. He figured the Mitchell brothers would use the thick cover to get in close. A faint light from the fire would assure them that their intended victim was sound asleep and easy to kill. Satisfied that he was well hidden, Byron settled down and waited. Two hours passed before he finally heard a rustle in the brush on the far side of the fire. He waited another five minutes, locating the outlines of men in the dark. When he finally saw the third one, he waited until all three were out in the open.

The air crackled with tension as one of the brothers unleashed a storm of bullets from his pistol. The muzzle flash seared Byron's vision, nearly blinding him. His bedroll jerked and twitched under the relentless impact of the shots. Meanwhile, the other brother joined in, adding to the hail of lead. The bedroll absorbed the punishment, its fabric rippling with each hit. Finally, the brothers ceased fire, lowering their pistols. Their attention shifted to the brush behind them, where the third man had remained hidden. Byron noted that these outlaws had deliberately stationed their comrades in the shadows, providing cover while they carried out their deadly intentions.

As the brothers approached Byron's bedroll, one delivered a swift kick, sending it skittering to the side. But something was amiss; the bedroll was far too light to conceal a body. Byron's instincts flared. "What the hell?" he muttered, realizing the encounter was far from over and survival hung in the balance.

The men, disoriented by Byron's unexpected retaliation, spun towards him. Swift and calculated, he aimed for the farthest figure, an old trick to sow confusion among his adversaries. The man emerging from the brush crumpled backwards, colliding against the undergrowth. Byron did not hesitate; he squeezed the trigger again before the others retaliated. The second man, the one who had kicked his bedroll, collapsed, but not without firing a desperate shot. Byron rolled to evade the third man's onslaught, gritting his teeth against the pain. Rising to one knee, he returned fire with two precise shots that found their mark. The wounded man staggered, his anguished cries echoing through the wilderness. Byron's resolve remained unyielding; he fired again, sending the assailant tumbling into the flames.

With only one bullet remaining in his pistol, Byron seized his rifle. Close-range engagements were not his preference, but necessity drove him. The first man to shoot groaned, rising from the bush where he'd fallen. Pistol in hand, he lunged towards Byron. Without hesitation, Byron's rifle spoke, and the man crumpled back into the foliage, the fight draining from him. Amidst the smoke and fading echoes, Byron stood as a lone survivor in a deadly game. His pulse steadied, but danger still lurked. The wilderness held its breath, awaiting the next move.

As the second man crumpled to the ground, a sudden burst of light erupted from his fading form, accompanied by the thunderous report of a heavy-caliber pistol. The lead projectile sliced through the air, grazing perilously close to Byron's head with a near-perfect shot. But Byron, ever vigilant, had anticipated this danger from the outset. His sideward movement spared him from the bullet's deadly trajectory. Byron swiftly dispatched the wounded man with two precise rifle rounds. The scene was enveloped in silence, broken only by the smell of roasted flesh and the lifeless body slumping into the fire. Death had claimed him.

After a tense ten-minute vigil, Byron finally departed. He moved with purpose, kneeling beside the last adversary he had shot. The man lay there with his eyes wide open, staring sightlessly at the moon above. Nearby, the wounded figure in the bush clung to life, though barely. His eyes tracked Byron's every move, yet no trace of a weapon remained on his person—only the fallen rifle lying a few feet away. The man's gaze bore into Byron, a silent plea or perhaps a final acknowledgment of defeat. Byron stood over the fallen man, the moment's weight settling upon him. The man's last breath escaped in a shudder, and then silence enveloped him. Byron's boot met flesh with a forceful kick, but the head merely lolled, life extinguished. The wilderness bore witness to the grim aftermath.

Methodically, Byron moved from one lifeless form to the next, reclaiming their weapons. His gear lay scattered, and he cursed as he discovered the bullet-riddled holes in his bedroll—a testament to the violent encounter. Swiftly, he saddled his horse, securing his belongings. With determination etched into his features, he mounted and rode off, covering several hundred yards before dismounting again to establish a makeshift camp. There was no fire this time; the night was warm, and the stars provided ample illumination. Byron settled onto his saddle, boots still on, and lay atop the bedroll. Fatigue and adrenaline battled within him as he dozed, waiting for the first light of dawn to reveal the path ahead.

As dawn's light painted the horizon, Byron again saddled his horse, the leather creaking under his practiced hands. He urged the horse into a slow canter, heading towards the eastern edge of the clearing. The sun had yet to emerge fully, casting a soft glow over the landscape. The scavenger buzzards had not yet descended upon the lifeless forms strewn across the ground. A few of them circled high above, but it was not just the predators that stirred.

As Byron approached the campsite, a low growl reached his ears. Hungry and opportunistic coyotes had gathered around what remained of the Mitchell brothers. Blood stained their muzzles, and primal hunger gleamed in their eyes. They quarreled over the grisly remains, their wiry bodies tense with anticipation. Byron's hand tightened around the grip of his pistol. He knew these scavengers well—their cunning and desperation. With a sharp crack, he fired several warning shots into the air. The coyotes scattered, yelping and darting into the underbrush. But one lingered; its jaws clamped around a severed hand, a grotesque trophy of their macabre banquet. Byron watched the lone coyote retreat, its eyes locking onto his. At that moment, he understood the harsh reality of survival in this unforgiving land. The dead Mitchell brothers were no longer a threat, but the living predators—humans and animals—could still be a danger, waiting for their chance.

Byron mounted his horse again, the morning's weight settling on him. He rode onward, leaving behind the remnants of violence and death, his resolve unyielding against the wilderness that tested him at every turn. However, the Mitchell brothers fared better than expected, and their injuries were not as severe as Byron might have feared. He methodically scoured the vicinity, riding in a wide circle until he stumbled upon their horses tied securely about a quarter mile away. The animals had remained saddled and bridled throughout the night. Deprived of any nearby sustenance due to their tethered confinement, they greeted Byron with relief and hunger.

Dismounting, Byron secured their lead ropes, remounted his horse, and skillfully guided the animals back to the campsite. But their unease grew palpable as the horses caught the scent of blood. Byron's nerves tightened; he urged them forward, the lash of a rope urging them on. Yet the tension escalated when they returned to the scene of the grim struggle. Amidst the fire's remnants, a lone coyote had reappeared. Its scavenging instincts drove it to gnaw at the remains of the man who had fallen into the flames. Annoyed by this audacity, Byron aimed and dispatched the animal with a single shot. The report echoed through the wilderness, startling the horses he led. Panic surged; they reared and bolted, their powerful muscles straining against Byron's desperate grip. In that chaotic moment, Byron grappled with the wild forces around him—the horses' primal fear, the lingering scent of death, and the relentless struggle for survival. His resolve held firm, but the wilderness remained unforgiving, testing him at every turn.

Byron's hands worked swiftly, securing the horses to sturdy bushes. The weight of the dead men's limp, blood-soaked bodies strained the animals. Their eyes widened, their nostrils flaring in alarm. But the lead ropes held firm. With grim determination, Byron loaded the lifeless bodies onto the saddles, lashing them into place. The horses shifted uneasily, their loyalty to their late masters warring with instinctive fear. Within half an hour, Byron led the trio of horses, each burdened with a corpse, towards the nearest town. Fortunately, it was conveniently along his route, just over thirty miles away.

As the morning sun climbed, he rode into the small settlement. The county seat boasted a sheriff's office, a sturdy building that stood out against the modest structures around it. Byron's arrival was noticed. Early drinkers spilled out of the saloons, glasses still in hand; their curiosity piqued. The lone barbershop emptied, its patrons drawn to the macabre spectacle. Byron dismounted, his boots thumping on the wooden boardwalk. The sheriff emerged, blinking in the daylight, only half comprehending the scene before him. Byron squared his shoulders, ready to face him.

"Come inside, Sheriff," he beckoned, hinting at a private matter for discussion.

The sheriff, taken aback by the sight of three lifeless bodies, couldn't help but exclaim in shock.

"The Mitchell brothers and their accomplice," Byron stated succinctly.

The sheriff, visibly astounded, approached to examine the bodies, now a gathering spot for flies, particularly around the moist areas of the eyes and mouths. Dispersing the flies with a wave of his hand, the sheriff scrutinised each face.

"I'll be damned, you're correct," he acknowledged, looking back at Byron, who gestured towards the jailhouse for a more private conversation.

Inside the cool adobe-brick building, the sheriff invited Byron to sit and took his place in a worn rocking chair beside his desk.

"What's on your mind?" he inquired, ready to get down to business.

"I'm with the U.S. Marshal's service," Byron began, cutting to the chase. "Those men outside tried to ambush me in my sleep. They failed miserably. As you're aware, there's a bounty of five hundred dollars per head on them, which adds up to a substantial sum."

The sheriff's eyes gleamed at the mention of money.

"Indeed, that's a significant amount," he concurred.

"Typically, the reward would be mine since I captured them. However, marshals aren't allowed to claim bounties," Byron explained, noticing the calculating look in the sheriff's eyes.

"That's true, but there's no rule against sheriffs claiming them," Byron proposed. "Let's say you were the one who took down those outlaws. You claim the reward and split it with me."

The sheriff, intrigued, asked about Byron's desired share. After a moment, Byron suggested an even split to avoid future complications. The sheriff was stunned by the offer of seven hundred and fifty dollars, a fortune compared to his modest monthly salary.

"I'd be a fool not to accept," he exclaimed.

Byron provided information about a Kansas City bank that transfers funds. The sheriff noted it down, further impressing Byron with his literacy. With nothing more to discuss, Byron prepared to leave. The sheriff stood, and Byron, fixing him with a firm gaze, insisted on the sheriff's commitment to send the money. The sheriff's fleeting hesitation vanished under Byron's unwavering stare, and he assured Byron of his intention to follow through. Byron then stepped outside and mounted his horse. He was riding out of town within minutes, heading east across the vast prairie.

11

HIS SKINNING KNIFE FINDING ITS MARK

Three days after encountering the sheriff, Byron neared Abigail's residence. Her home was in a secluded spot, a good ten miles from the closest small town and fifty miles from the bustling streets of Kansas City. The Shield Homestead sprawled over a quarter of land, where she raised horses and a modest number of cattle. Her only consistent help came from an elderly hand named Joseph. She would employ temporary workers during busier times, like the roundup or when breaking in new horses. Abigail stood out as one of the most fiercely independent women Byron had ever encountered, her self-reliance bordering on recklessness. It troubled him that she chose to live in such isolation, with only old Joseph for company on the fringes of the wilderness. He had voiced his concerns to her several times, to which she would retort, "If you don't want me to be lonely, why not stay a while longer?"

Such an invitation was out of character for Abigail, a woman who generally kept men at arm's length. Her past marriage to a charming yet unreliable gambler had left her wary; he was a handsome cardsharp who had a habit of running off with other women, only to return to Abigail when he was broke or in trouble. But one fateful night, his luck ran out during a card game with three buffalo hunters. Having gambled away his last dime, Abigail's husband staked his wife as his final bet. The buffalo hunters, who had spotted Janet earlier, readily accepted.

"Agreed," declared one of the hunters, a towering figure with unkempt black hair and buckskins caked in the grime of countless hunts.

As Abigail's husband triumphantly laid down a full house, expecting to claim the pot, one hunter interjected, spreading out his cards to reveal a king-high straight flush. The husband's momentary shock quickly turned to despair and rage, for despite his faults, he truly loved

Abigail. In a desperate move, he reached for his hidden pistol. But the hunter was quicker, his skinning knife finding its mark in the gambler's chest before the pistol was even drawn. With a swift kick, the hunter cleared the dying man from the table, gathered his winnings, and signalled to his companions.

"Time to collect our winnings," he said gruffly.

Byron learned of the grim events a few hours later. He had met Abigail before and was struck by her independence. He had even begun to fall for her, puzzled by her attachment to a man he deemed unworthy. Byron had once questioned her choice, and she had confessed her growing doubts about her life with him. Byron, a man not usually inclined towards lasting commitments, contemplated making a serious offer to Abigail. She captivated him more than any other woman had. Her beauty was striking at twenty-four, a blend of dark flowing hair, a radiant, intelligent countenance, and a physique hinting at grace and vitality. Yet her indomitable spirit drew him to her self-sufficiency, her sharp mind, and the undeniable allure of her presence.

Byron was incensed upon learning of the appalling bet her husband had made. The buffalo hunters had been brave, claiming Abigail as their prize at her doorstep. Defiant, Abigail had resisted, but they overpowered her, abducting her from her home. As they vanished into the vastness of the prairie with Abigail in tow, Byron knew he had to act, driven by a newfound purpose beyond mere attraction.

As soon as Byron grasped the gravity of the situation, he hastily gathered his belongings and made his way to the stable. With swift movements, he prepared his horse for the pursuit. Moments later, he was galloping out of town, hot on the trail of the abductors. His steed was solid and fast, and the tracks indicated that Abigail was fighting, trying to hinder the hunters' progress. As dusk approached, Byron spotted the group of four silhouettes against the fading light, about two miles in the distance. He urged his horse forward, narrowing the distance between them. However, the hunters had noticed him, and he realised he couldn't get any closer without risking a confrontation. The buffalo hunters were armed with formidable Sharps rifles, known for their long-range accuracy. While hitting a moving target was more challenging than shooting a stationary buffalo, it wasn't impossible. Sensing their intent to set up an ambush, Byron watched through his binoculars as several hunters dismounted. Even from afar, he could make out the ominous shape of their rifles, propped up on tripods, ready for a deadly standoff.

Byron stowed his binoculars and calmly redirected his horse, opting for a strategic retreat. Meanwhile, the hunters carefully prepared their rifles, anchoring their shooting sticks firmly into the earth. They adjusted the rifles' long barrels onto the sticks' forked rests and raised the leaf sights, gauging the distance at about a thousand yards. Aiming at a moving target like Byron, now retreating at an oblique angle, posed a challenge. Nonetheless, the hunters took their time, and when they were ready, one after another, they took their shots.

Byron's quick thinking and agile manoeuvres saved him from the hunters' bullets. As he glanced back, he saw the tell-tale white smoke of their rifles. The sound of a fifty-calibre bullet zipping past, kicking up a cloud of dirt, urged him to act fast. He spurred his horse into a swift run, weaving back and forth to make himself a more challenging target. He knew the hunters' aim might not reach him, but a stray bullet could injure his horse and end the pursuit. With a firm press of his spurs, he pushed his mount into a full gallop, continuing his zigzag pattern. Within moments, he had disappeared from the hunters' view, putting distance between him and the danger. The chase was far from over, and Byron was determined to rescue Abigail from her captors.

Byron recognised the buffalo hunters' determination and knew they wouldn't give up their claim without a struggle. Accustomed to the harshness of their trade, they were likely to continue, especially with a follower in pursuit. With this knowledge, Byron steeled himself for what was to come. He understood that a battle might be necessary to rescue Abigail and was prepared to take that risk. His determination was as unwavering as the prairie wind that hinted at the looming conflict. Byron was set to confront whatever challenges lay before him in his quest to save her.

As night enveloped the prairie, Byron relied on his mount's endurance, veering left in a wide arc to outflank the hunters. For three gruelling hours, he urged his horse on, aware that time was of the essence for Abigail's well-being. His vigilance paid off when he spotted a campfire's glow in the distance. With cautious manoeuvres, he approached, utilising the terrain's dips and hollows to remain unseen against the sparse moonlight. At a discreet distance of a hundred yards, Byron paused, surveying the campsite keenly and strategising his next move in the silent darkness. The rescue was within reach, but the final approach had to be calculated with precision.

Amidst the flickering firelight, three horses stood near the campfire. Two men were visible, along with a woman—Abigail. She crouched, half-naked, her dress torn from shoulders to waist, defiantly facing two buffalo hunters. Strangely absent were the third hunter and his horse. Byron arrived just in time; the hunters had barely begun their cruel work on the girl. Abigail's clenched fists and taut expression revealed her determination despite her vulnerable position. Eyes widened as he noticed the rope tied around her right ankle. One of the hunters held the other end, exerting force. Suddenly, Abigail's right leg shot out from under her, and she fell hard onto her back. The other man pounced, attempting to pin her down, but Abigail fought back fiercely. Byron winced as he witnessed a brutal backhand across her face. For a moment, she lay still, allowing the second man to close in, parting her legs. Darkness enveloped them as desperation and violence unfolded in the fire's wavering glow.

Byron hesitated, torn between urgency and caution. The elusive third man remained a threat; if he lurked beyond the fire's glow, rifle in hand, Byron's advance would be met with a deadly bullet. But then, a glimmer of hope: movement in the brush on the fire's far side. A horse and rider materialised from the darkness. The man's blade gleamed in the firelight, balanced on his thigh.

"Goddamn it!" he cursed. "You boys are trying to hog it all while I freeze my arse off in the weeds."

Abigail's plight intensified the tension. The man who had been restraining her thighs sprang into action.

"Stay alert!" he barked at the horseman. "That son of a bitch could be anywhere, sneaking up on us right now."

Indeed, the third man approached from an unexpected angle. Byron edged his horse forward, aiming for proximity before discovery. Abigail's struggle diverted their attention. Amidst their argument, she seized an opportunity and bolted for the brush. The rope-bound man tripped her once more, dragging her back while the other pursued. The mounted man's laughter echoed—a cruel soundtrack to the desperate struggle unfolding in the darkness.

Byron's decisive moment unfolded in the moonlit chaos. Thirty yards from the fire, he spurred his horse, galloping towards Abigail and the menacing duo. The rhythmic hoofbeats echoed, but time had betrayed the hunters. Byron emerged from the shadows astride his steed, determination etched on his face, a hefty Remington pistol clenched. His aim was swift; the man with the knife fell first, a single gunshot shattering the night.

The other assailant, atop Janet, sprang up, panic in his eyes. His unfastened trousers tangled with Abigail's desperate pull, throwing him off balance. Byron closed the gap, riding alongside him, and fired into the man's chest. The impact sent him sprawling. Yet danger loomed. The mounted man, rifle raised, had Byron in his sights. But close-quarters combat with a lengthy barrel, especially with a buffalo gun, had drawbacks. The bullet whizzed past Byron, searing the air, missing by a mere inch or two. Flesh stung from the near miss, and adrenaline surged. In that fateful moment, Byron's resolve held firm—a dance of life and death under the moon's watchful gaze.

The Sharps rifle, a single-shot breech-loader, lay discarded. The buffalo hunter wrestled with the breech, ejecting the spent shell casing, desperate to reload. But Byron bore down on him, determination etched in every stride. The hunter abandoned the rifle, reaching for his pistol. Byron's shot rang out before the hunter could retaliate, yet the man stood firm, a hulking figure of defiance. Grimacing, he cocked the pistol's hammer, but Byron fired once more, sending him sprawling over the horse's rear. The moon watched, silent witness to this brutal dance of survival.

Despite the barrage of bullets, the tenacious man clung to life, refusing to release his pistol. Byron fired twice more, each shot echoing through the tense night. He was stretched thin. Byron pivoted his mount, realising that his pistol must be empty. Meanwhile, one of the bandits, trousers tangled around his ankle, crawled towards the discarded weapon, which he had dropped when Byron first wounded him. Byron urged his horse forward, abandoning the pistol and seizing the rifle's butt. But fate intervened. Abigail, fuelled by anger and hatred, lunged at the crawling man. Her impact sent them both sprawling, their struggle a desperate tangle of limbs. Abigail clung to the man, legs wrapped around his body, thwarting his reach for the pistol. Byron, rifle in hand, hesitated. Shooting risked hitting Abigail. Darkness enveloped them, and the moon bore witness to this chaotic survival dance.

Byron didn't need to fire another shot. Abigail, still clinging to the man's back, had wrested his skinning knife from its sheath at the back of his belt. Unaware that it was the very blade that had taken her husband's life, she wielded it with a desperate determination. In the firelight, the blade gleamed—a beacon of vengeance. It arced high, then descended, tearing into the man's chest. His scream echoed through the night as he dropped his pistol, attempting to dislodge Abigail. But she held on, the knife rising and falling, its once-reflective surface now stained crimson. She must have stabbed him a dozen times before Byron dismounted and gently took hold of her hand. The man lay beneath her, eyes ablaze with horror, the last vestiges of breath escaping his gasping mouth.

Abigail's wrist twisted under the unfamiliar touch, her expression fierce as she confronted Byron. For a heartbeat, it seemed a brawl might erupt. Then recognition dawned in her eyes, extinguishing the fire of battle.

"Oh God," she half-whispered, trembling.

Byron enveloped her in his arms, acutely aware of her dishevelled attire; the fabric was torn and stained. Her bare skin pressed against his, a raw intimacy born of shared danger. Her shudders rippled through her, and he assumed she wept silently. Yet, when she raised her face, only two solitary tear tracks marred the dirt. Blood coated her, but Byron's swift assessment prevailed that little, if any, belonged to her. The moon bore witness to their fragile reunion, a survivor's embrace amidst the aftermath of violence.

Abigail surveyed the grim aftermath of the camp—the lifeless bodies sprawled around her. Her gaze then settled on Byron, a determined look in her eyes. For a fleeting moment, she attempted to adjust her torn dress, a futile effort to regain modesty. But urgency overrode embarrassment. She met Byron's gaze squarely.

"I want to get out of here. Now."

Byron wasted no time. He strode to where the buffalo hunters' horses were tethered. He reserved the best one for Abigail, saddling the others swiftly. The blankets strewn on the ground held no appeal; they were filthy and infested with lice. Instead, he draped his coat over her shoulders, assisting her onto the horse. Together, they rode into the night, leaving the fallen hunters to scavengers and coyotes.

Guiding her only a few miles away, Byron led Abigail to the bank of a small stream he had passed earlier. Dismounting, he tended to the horses and kindled a fire. Meanwhile, Abigail disappeared into the darkness, drawn towards the stream's soothing murmur. Byron listened to the splashing water, waiting. When she returned, his coat still clung to her shoulders, but now it was clean, a stark contrast to the blood that had once stained her. The moon bore witness to their escape, and a fragile Byron carefully opened a can of hash; its contents warmed over the glowing coals.

Abigail hesitated, her hunger warring with exhaustion. But when he spooned a small portion onto a makeshift plate, she relented. Ravenously, she devoured the rest. Her eyes drooped, weariness etching lines on her face.

"I'm tired," she murmured, her voice fragile. "I want so very much to sleep."

The fire crackled, casting shadows on their refuge—a fragile haven in the wilderness. The chill of dawn settled around them, and Byron carefully spread out his bedroll near the crackling fire. It was sturdy, fashioned from an old overcoat and assorted scraps, meticulously sewn together into a cosy pouch. The oilskin covering offered protection against rain—a thoughtful touch. He watched as the girl hesitated, hoping she would accept the makeshift bedding. In a few days, he planned to clean it thoroughly, leaving it near an anthill to let the diligent ants rid it of lingering pests—an ancient Indian trick.

As the girl shed the remnants of her tattered, bloodstained clothing, Byron averted his gaze. Naked, she slipped into the bedroll. On the other side of the fire, he lay on the cold ground, his saddle blanket providing minimal comfort. She was silent for ten minutes until the girl's voice pierced the night.

"They told me they killed my husband," she said, her eyes searching his. "Is that true?"

Byron's hesitation hung in the air, a weighty acknowledgement. "I'm afraid it is," he finally replied, his voice carrying the burden of truth.

Abigail's response was a simple, "Oh," her voice fragile, as if the revelation had drained her.

Minutes passed, and the fire was crackling in the stillness. Then Abigail's voice trembled, revealing her vulnerability.

"I'm cold. I'm scared. I'm lonely." Her plea cut through the night. "I want you to get in here with me."

Byron hesitated once more, torn between duty and compassion.

"Please," she implored, her words almost swallowed by the darkness.

It was a moment of raw need—the first and last time he heard her sound so utterly lost. Resolute, he rose. Crossing the space, he settled near the bedroll, boots discarded and gun belt placed carefully aside. Gently, he slid inside, Janet making room for him. Her skin met his, and she whispered, "Your belt buckle is hurting my skin."

In that fragile cocoon of shared warmth, they sought solace—a fragile haven against the harsh world beyond. Byron hesitated briefly, then climbed out of the bedroll and removed all his clothing. As he settled back into the bedroll, he keenly felt the warmth of her exposed skin brushing against his. She pressed herself against him, her face mere inches from his own. He could discern her open eyes, studying his features. Her arms encircled him, pulling him closer. Her legs opened so that his knee ended up between her thighs.

"Well, I'll be goddamned," he muttered, his hand tentatively moving over her breasts, aware of the hardness of the nipples and the rapid panting of her breath against his ear.

Her lovemaking was wild, almost savage. Byron had seen it happen before with other women, when, after facing danger and in the presence of death, an overwhelming urge to make love, to reassure life, swept over them. This was as intense a reaction as any he had seen. He and the girl made love again and again until finally, with a satisfied little sound coming from way back in her throat, Abigail fell asleep.

After mending her dress the following day, she regained modest coverage. Together, they retraced their steps towards town. That day, she radiated vitality, casting warm glances in Byron's direction. She engaged in lively conversation, sharing details about her husband. She had wed him at a tender age, captivated by his handsome appearance and eloquent speech. Hailing from a reasonably affluent family, she felt stifled by their rigidity. However, her Bible-thumping father's inappropriate advances, fuelled by months of observing her youthful figure, prompted her to realise her days at home were limited. This realisation suited her well as she eagerly awaited her future husband's arrival. In her naivety, she had fervently pushed for marriage, a decision she would later rue. The mere fact of their marital bond held significance for her, perhaps influenced by her upbringing. Despite any provocations, severing ties with the man proved arduous. She clung to the union even after swiftly realising his overall lack of value. As they returned to town, Byron sensed an inexplicable familiarity with Abigail.

Conversation flowed effortlessly between them, a novel experience for Byron, who had always grappled with unease during social interactions. Unbeknownst to him, loneliness had been creeping into his life. He'd been partnered with Dr Tommy Cree for three years, a man starkly dissimilar to Byron. Tommy hailed from an Eastern background, exuding education, sartorial elegance, and a penchant for grandiloquent language. This combination often grated on Byron's nerves. Yet fate intervened when the audacious Tommy wed a wealthy woman, leaving Byron to traverse trails and campsites in solitary contemplation.

Upon their return to town, Byron faced a barrage of curious questions from the locals. At the same time, Abigail ascended to her room, where she exchanged her attire for another dress. The local undertaker had already prepared her husband's lifeless form, and this time, the undertaker was overjoyed to be paid for tending to the latest saloon casualty.

The funeral took place that very afternoon. Abigail stood by the graveside, her expression pensive, perhaps even tinged with sadness. Byron remained silent, observing the proceedings. After the brief funeral, Janet gathered her scant belongings and prepared to depart from town. Outside her room, Byron intercepted her.

"Are you returning home?" he asked.

"I don't have a home," Abigail replied. "Not yet."

"Are you actively seeking one?" Byron probed.

"Maybe," she answered, meeting his gaze. "And will you assist me in this quest?"

"Maybe," Byron echoed.

Together, they rode out of town, their path leading eastward. The open road held uncertainty and possibility, and as they ventured forth, their fates intertwined.

12

ABIGAIL EMERGED ONTO THE PORCH

Over a year had passed, and Byron found himself once again riding towards the spot where Abigail had chosen to make her home. She insisted on living independently, away from other people, except for Byron himself. His work often took him away, leaving Abigail alone in this rugged land without the safety of a nearby town. Despite his concerns, he suspected that Abigail's desire for solitude was her way of coping with her encounter with the buffalo hunters. Therefore, he left her there with Joseph for extended periods. Yet, when they were together, their connection remained intense. Abigail's passion for Byron was as evident as his own for her. Initially, he had expected her to ask him to abandon his work and stay with her, as most couples would. But Abigail surprised him. When he broached the topic, she declined, understanding that Byron was not suited for a settled, sedentary life. Despite the challenges of their separation, their reunions were the highlight of their lives.

The dog was the first to notice him. The barking alerted old Joseph, who shuffled onto the porch, squinting his dim eyes. Now sure that it was Byron, Joseph hurried to the front door, shouting inside that the humble man had returned home again. Byron dismounted at the hitching rail, and Abigail emerged onto the porch as he swung down from his horse. The telltale signs were there: she must have been working with the colts again, clad in a pair of men's dungarees, their fabric stiff from horse sweat.

"Byron!" she exclaimed in that wonderfully uninhibited manner of hers. Without hesitation, she leapt off the porch and flung herself into his arms. Joseph discreetly vanished for the next few hours, allowing Byron and Abigail to rekindle their connection.

Their encounter was intense, spanning two passionate hours. It began with a hug near the porch. It culminated in the large double bed that Abigail had transported from

Kansas City. Now, both naked and exhausted, they were ready for conversation. Curious about Byron's whereabouts, Abigail asked, "Where have you been?"

His response was straightforward: "Mostly in Wyoming, up around Jackson Hole, and then down to Cheyenne."

Abigail sensed his discontent and probed further. "You don't sound too pleased with whatever you were doing."

Byron's reply was succinct: "Nope. It involved dirty work. Some things a man shouldn't have to do."

Byron glanced at Abigail, admiring her beauty. Their passionate encounter had flushed her face, and her dark, damp hair clung to her neck and shoulders. He noticed that her body had become slightly leaner since their initial meeting. The colts' wildness could indeed leave a mark on a person, but despite that, an abundance of women remained nearby. And her howl was such a visceral response. The advice echoed in his mind: "If you don't like it, drop it." He pondered momentarily, then admitted, "Well, yeah."

The idea took root, growing silently within him. "Yeah, maybe," he murmured, gazing into the distance.

"Maybe what?" Abigail demanded, playfully poking him.

His face lit up with animation. "Let's get the hell out of here," he proposed. "Just take off. The two of us head to California. I've been there before and liked it well enough, at least to take a look at. We could drive up to San Francisco. That was maybe Doc's favourite town, you know. Then, when it gets a little colder, we could head down to the southern part of Santa Barbara and Los Angeles. Although the area is quite sparsely populated, it is certainly cosy and warm during the winter. They grow oranges there. We could pick them off the trees and spend a few months just doing whatever the hell we want to do."

Abigail chuckled. "You're talking like a rich man."

Byron grinned. "Well," he replied, "I am rich, kind of."

Byron shared details of the Mitchell brothers' and the rule boards' anticipated arrival at the Kansas City bank with Abigail. They could weather some prosperous times by combining his existing three hundred dollars, Abigail's resources, and his back pay. Surprisingly, Abigail refrained from teasing him about his musings. The allure of nest-building was waning for her; breaking horses had become more pragmatic than enjoyable. Her memories of the buffalo hunters had faded into near invisibility. But Abigail's eagerness sparked a new possibility.

"I think we could do it," she declared. Joseph's family from Mexico had two sons, and their families could manage the place while they were away. The opportunity was ripe, and Joseph needed additional assistance due to his advancing age. Janet's enthusiasm was contagious: "Let's do it, Byron!"

And with that decisive word, the die was cast. "Done."

In the upcoming days, they were buzzing with enthusiastic planning. Their journey would commence by riding the train to California, and then, once there, they'd rely mostly on horseback for travel. Byron considered himself fortunate to have a woman like Abigail, someone who appreciated the rugged, earthbound style of travel where you could genuinely connect with the land beneath your feet. Imagining Abigail riding beside him filled him with immense satisfaction.

However, practical matters loomed. The money they had would eventually dwindle. Meanwhile, Joseph's sons and their families were expected to arrive by month's end. Byron embarked on a journey to Kansas City as the last week of the month approached. His mission was to check if the reward money had been deposited in the bank. If not, he'd ride west and persuade a sheriff to grant him his rightful share.

The upcoming days were buzzing with enthusiastic planning. Their journey would commence by riding the train to California. Once there, they'd rely mostly on horseback for travel. Byron considered himself fortunate to have a woman like Abigail, someone who appreciated the rugged, earthbound style of travel where you could genuinely connect with the land beneath your feet. Imagining Abigail riding beside him filled him with joy. However, practical matters loomed. The money they had would eventually dwindle. Byron pondered what kind of work he could do to allow him to remain close to Abigail.

Meanwhile, Joseph's sons and their families were expected to arrive by month's end. Byron embarked on a journey to Kansas City as the last week of the month approached. His mission was to check if the reward money had been deposited in the bank. If not, he'd ride west and persuade a sheriff to grant him his rightful share.

Joseph's sons and their families were expected to arrive by the end of the month. As the last week of the month began, Byron embarked on a journey to Kansas City. He aimed to verify whether the reward money had been deposited in the bank. If it hadn't, he planned to ride west and persuade a sheriff to grant him his share. Byron took his time along the way, not arriving in Kansas City until the evening of the second day. He secured a room in a small hotel and was at the bank promptly the following day. To his relief, the money had indeed arrived.

Byron requested it in banknotes and gold coins. The bank also handled Janet's account, and she had given

Byron a draft to cash. The bank manager recognised them both. He was a talkative man, and he soon attempted to engage Byron in conversation. Byron responded absently, but his attention was suddenly caught by something the bank manager had just mentioned.

"What's that?" he inquired. "Some men were asking for me."

"Uh-uh," the bank manager confirmed. "Indeed, they were. They claimed to be good friends, saying they had met you during your work."

Byron's mind raced, unable to locate any friends who were privy to his bank account. Who were these men?

The bank manager, sensing Byron's unease, hesitated before responding. "Well," he began, "they were a strangely eclectic group. One of them, the dominant figure, was remarkably cultured and a fascinating conversationalist. We delved into discussions about banking practices; he was remarkably knowledgeable."

However, the other two were quite different, rough around the edges and cut from coarser cloth. I'm almost embarrassed to admit that they worked for him."

Byron pressed further. "Their names," he insisted. "I need to know what names they were using."

Byron's mind raced, unable to think of any friends who were privy to his bank account. Who were these men? He demanded more details about their appearance. The bank manager, sensing Byron's unease, hesitated before responding.

"Well," he began, "they were a strangely eclectic group. One of them, the dominant figure, was remarkably cultured and a fascinating conversationalist. We delved into discussions about banking practices; he was remarkably knowledgeable. However, the other two were quite different, rough around the edges and cut from coarser cloth. I'm almost embarrassed to admit that they worked for him."

Byron pressed further. "Their names," he insisted. "I need to know what names they were using."

The bank manager hesitated, then replied, "Honestly, I'm unsure if they provided names. But never mind that. Let me tell you where they went."

Byron's pulse quickened as the bank manager's words sank in. Who were these men, and why were they looking out for him? The urgency of the situation propelled him into action.

"Directions?" Byron's voice was sharp, and his gaze was unwavering.

Byron's anger flared. "Ah, you goddamned fool!" he snarled. Without waiting for a response, he stormed out of the bank, his boots echoing on the wooden floor. He swiftly made his way to the stables, effortlessly mounting his horse. Five minutes later, he was galloping out of town like a man possessed, driving the animal mercilessly. Daniel van de Velt, Boulder Ross, and Dean Phillips raced through his mind. The bank manager's description fit them perfectly. The thought of those three heading for Abigail's place turned his stomach. He had to reach her before they did.

Later that afternoon, Byron had to reduce his pace; his horse showed fatigue. He allowed the animal a brief rest, then pushed forward. As he approached the house, the horse was on the verge of collapse. Dismounting two hundred yards shy of the house, Byron concealed himself in a small grove of trees. The dying horse gasped its last breath nearby as Byron continued on foot, moving swiftly but silently. He gripped his revolver tightly, his heart pounding.

"God, let everything be all right!" he prayed. "May they not have arrived here?"

However, it was far from all right. Old Joseph lay half-buried beneath the porch, two gunshot wounds to his chest. An ancient musket ball clung to the older man's lifeless hand in a futile attempt at resistance. Throwing caution aside, Byron raced through the house, searching desperately. Yet the rooms were empty, and the building was devoid of life. Abigail was nowhere to be found.

Byron descended the stairs, his eyes scanning the living room. A note was laid on a low table next to Janet's cherished couch. He hadn't noticed it during his initial pass through the room, but now it demanded his attention. Scooping up the paper, he read its contents with growing dread:

> Byron, sorry, we missed you. While the trip wasn't entirely in vain, we're grateful for the chance to meet the charming young woman who resides here. I suspect she holds significant value for you. How fitting. I understand you've had the good fortune of spending time with my wife and children. Now, it's time to repay your kindness. We have taken the girl with us. If you wish, follow along. We will do our best to leave fragments of her along the trail.

Daniel van de Velt

As if Byron hadn't already known the name. His heart raced, and a sickening realisation settled in. Abigail was in danger, and he had to act swiftly. The note had emphasised the trail, and Byron knew he had to follow it.

Urgently, he sprinted towards the corrals. Van de Velt and the others had already taken most of the better horses, but one animal remained—a weary-looking steed capable of carrying him. Within minutes, he had it saddled and bridled, then galloped out of the yard without a backward glance.

As he rode, Van de Velt's ominous words echoed in Byron's mind: "Bits and pieces of Abigail, along the trail." He scrutinised the ground, half-expecting to encounter gruesome remnants. Yet, there were none except for Abigail's scarf, hanging from a branch like a cryptic signpost. Perhaps she or Van de Velt had deliberately placed it there, ensuring he noticed where they'd veered off the main trail.

Byron's horse gave out in the middle of the night. In the distance, he heard a dog barking. He pounded on the door, guiding the stumbling animal towards an isolated farmhouse. The startled farmer nearly shot him, but eventually, the new horse was a sorry nag, already wearing on Byron. Just after dawn, he spotted an old house perched on a hill about a mile away. Despite the darkness, he had followed the trail, gambling that his quarry would continue in a straight line. Now, with daylight revealing the path, he saw that they had indeed done so; the tracks led directly towards the house.

Byron approached cautiously, the place appearing deserted. No horses were tied up outside, and the signs of occupancy were nonexistent. Existentially, he considered moving on, convinced they had merely rested here before continuing their journey. Then he noticed something near one of the windows. Byron jerked his horse to the side, reaching for his Remington. But as he focused, he realised it was only a piece of cloth hanging half out of the window and fluttering in the morning breeze. It took him a second to recognise it as a fragment of a dress he had seen Abigail wear many times—the same dress she wore when doing chores.

Byron dismounted hastily and rushed into the house. His eyes went straight to the cloth, which lay by itself, draped over the windowsill. He continued his search, always moving to make himself a difficult target. As he passed a door leading into another room, he finally saw Abigail.

Abigail lay naked on a stained mattress, carelessly tossed onto the floor. The pool of blood surrounding her was a grim indicator that she was lifeless. Byron, however, clung to desperation. He knelt beside the mattress, gazing into her vacant eyes, and softly called her, "Abigail."

There was no response, only the echo of the deceased and the hum of flies congregating near the blood. Byron laid a hand on her arm, recoiling from the flesh's frigid, damp lifelessness and grotesque nature. Then, propelled by fury, he sprang to his feet and tore through the house, bellowing, "Van de Velt! Show yourself, you wretched scoundrel! Reveal your presence, and I shall scatter your entrails across these walls like an owl's macabre art!"

No response echoed, only a profound silence. Byron dashed outdoors, scouring the underbrush near the house. Yet nothing but faint tracks led into the distance.

Returning to the house proved agonising for Byron. Summoning his resolve, he stepped into the room with the mattress, deliberately avoiding the remnants of Abigail. After a minute or two, his eyes fell upon a note beneath the bed. He stooped, retrieved it, and read the words etched upon it:

US Marshal, once again, extends gratitude for allowing us to acquaint ourselves with your intended. We came to know her intimately before she chose to depart. I thank you, and Loss extends its thanks as well. And on behalf of my wife, I express my gratitude.

The note, intended to wound, had indeed struck its mark. As he shifted his gaze from the note to Abigail's lifeless, mutilated form, its words seeped into Byron's consciousness. Yet Van de Velt's utterances bore a more profound impact. They ignited an incendiary thirst for vengeance and a searing determination to exact retribution within Byron.

"You're a dead man, Van de Velt," he whispered, the words barely audible. "And you, too, Loss. Phillips; all of you prepare to meet your demise, and may it be brutal."

13

FORCED HIM INTO UNCHARACTERISTIC SITUATIONS

Abigail's clothing lay in tatters, rendering it impossible to dress her again. Byron discovered an aged blanket in another room and gently wrapped her lifeless form. As he lifted her, her head lolled, and her body hung heavily. Avoiding eye contact with his burden, Byron stepped out of the house. His horse shifted restlessly as he hoisted the bloodied corpse onto the saddle, but exhaustion dulled the animal's protests. With Abigail now securely bound in place, Byron's gaze was compelled down the trail where Van de Velt and the others had ridden. The imprints of their horses' hooves marked the path.

Suppressing his fatigue, Byron acknowledged that his horse lacked the stamina to pursue them swiftly. And then there was Abigail's desire to return home, to the sanctuary where safety once embraced her. Strangely,

Byron reflected on their shared history; he had rescued her from a similar fate. Yet he wondered if this was Abigail's destined end. His earlier intervention had postponed the inevitable; it hadn't thwarted it.

Byron retraced his steps, leading the horse. The exhausted animal couldn't bear the weight of both of them. After covering about a mile, Byron's feet throbbed painfully. His boots, designed with high heels and pointed toes, were ill-suited for walking. As a horseman, he typically avoided walking whenever possible, even if the distance was less than one hundred yards. Yet, the demands of his work had occasionally forced him into uncharacteristic situations, so he was prepared. He retrieved a pair of moccasins from his saddlebags and swapped them for the boots. Even with the moccasins, walking proved challenging. Sharp stones bruised his feet, and muscles unaccustomed to such exertion began to ache.

Byron welcomed the discomfort, accepting the humiliation of being on foot. He recognised his guilt, at least in part, for Abigail's demise. He had numerous opportunities to eliminate the boss and the others, but fear held him back. He played it safe, rationalising his hesitance to act swiftly. Now that Abigail was lost, he grappled with his characteristic timidity. Strangely, Abigail herself had once formed a bond with him, and perhaps her absence now revealed the true nature of his hesitation. Byron wrestled with the weight of their relationship, its profound significance, and the unbearable thought of never seeing her again. This fear of loss paralysed him, stifling his freedom and spontaneity. And tragically, it was this very hesitation that sealed Abigail's fate. He hadn't acted swiftly enough to eliminate the killers, allowing them to remain alive and dangerous.

But now, fuelled by rage and grief, Byron resolved to avenge Abigail. Time blurred as he pressed forward, pausing briefly during the night to rest on the ground and snatch a few hours of sleep. As dawn approached, he glimpsed the location where he had left the horse, now carrying Abigail's lifeless form. Approaching the farmhouse, the farmer's eyes widened at the conspicuous cords securing Byron's mount. Yet, any concern turned to delight when Byron offered his horse in exchange for fifty dollars, with an additional twenty thrown in for a battered old saddle. The urgency of his mission drove him forward, pushing aside regret and propelling him towards justice.

Byron remounted, making significantly better time as he arrived back at the house late that afternoon. His expectation was grim: Abigail's body was likely half-devoured by scavengers. However, the position of the bodies, particularly Abigail's, partially sheltered under the porch, seemed to have offered some protection. Joseph, though emitting a putrid odour, remained relatively intact. Byron carefully unlatched Abigail from the saddle and gently laid her on the porch. The stench was beginning to envelop her too, but Byron deliberately pushed those thoughts aside.

He tended to the horses, unsaddling them and leading them into the corral. Then, motivated by purpose, he headed to the barn to retrieve a shovel. About fifty yards from the house, a small knoll lay where Abigail had often sat, watching sunsets. Byron ascended the knoll and began digging two graves. Lamplight illuminated his sad task, and eventually, he fashioned two deep, dark pits in the earth. Without delay, he placed the bodies in their final resting places, leaving them uncovered until daylight. Nearby, he lay on the ground, dozing intermittently, his .44 revolver within reach, ever vigilant against scavengers that might disturb the solemn peace of the graves.

As the sun's first warm rays caressed the earth piled around the graves, Byron cast a handful of flowers directly onto Abigail's blanket-wrapped corpse. The time had been too scarce for formal offerings. Next, he gently placed Joseph's old, worn-out pistol atop his remains, murmuring, "You tried, old man. You did your best."

Byron lingered, lost in thought and memories, before meticulously filling the graves. Another day passed, spent nearby, seeking solace. The house held too many reminders of Abigail, making sleep within its walls unbearable. The following day, he rode into the small town where Abigail had filed her land papers with the local lawyer. Byron suspected she had family somewhere, and perhaps they deserved to know. However, when he informed the lawyer, a man who seemed perpetually on the brink of drunkenness, Byron received surprising news. Abigail had recently drawn up a will, bequeathing the land and all her possessions to him. There was no mention of family.

Byron returned to the house, the weight of ownership pressing on his shoulders. As he neared, an unexpected sight greeted him: people clustered around an old, weathered wagon parked by the porch. For an instant, Byron's mind flashed to the last visitor, Van de Velt, and the others. He spurred his horse into a run, his face contorting into a snarl. Yet, as he galloped towards the yard, pistol in hand, he startled not the killers but a Mexican family. They followed him with wary eyes. A few questions revealed that the daughter of two sons had finally arrived with their families. Suspicion hung in the air, even among the little children. They noticed the graves and sensed the house's desolation. Something was amiss.

Byron shared the grim news: Joseph was dead. The woman's wails filled the air, and tears flowed freely. The men, more composed, held their emotions inward, their innate dignity shielding them from revealing too much vulnerability to a stranger. Together, they assisted Byron in crafting grave markers, a solemn task that etched the memory of those lost.

As Joseph's family prepared to move on, signs of their readiness were evident. Their destination remained uncertain; they were clearly at the end of their resources. For Byron, this presented an opportunity to sever the last ties to his belongings, the remnants of his connection to Abigail. He insisted that the two men accompany him into town, where he formally transferred ownership of the house and a quarter section of land to them. The men, taken aback by this unexpected act of generosity, hesitated. But Byron cut through their objections:

"Don't get on your high horse. This land is not coming from me or even the Senora, who once lived here. It's coming from your father, Joseph. He died defending it. That makes it as much yours as anyone's in my book."

Eventually, Joseph's family accepted this unexpected gift. Their earlier destitution had left them in a precarious situation, but now they found themselves possessing more land than they had ever imagined. As Byron rode away, their blessings echoed behind him, accompanying him down the trail. With no burdens weighing him down, Abigail lay to rest on her land, and the land passed on. Byron was free to fulfil the vow he had made as he gazed upon his lover's lifeless body. Revenge against Abigail's murderers beckoned—a fate he had postponed but not thwarted.

14

PURSUING VAN DE VELT

Byron reached the nearest railhead and purchased a train ticket bound for Chicago, where Gardiner had established an agency headquarters. Before boarding the train, Byron decided to sell his current mount, anticipating the need for a better horse in the future. After inspecting his saddle, bridle, and saddlebags, he stowed them in the baggage cart. He carried his bedroll under one arm, his Winchester rifle in hand, and made his way to the second-class car. The US marshals and operatives, who contributed significantly to the railroads' operations, were regularly granted free railway passes. These passes typically gave access to second-class accommodations, which didn't bother Byron. As he settled onto the hard wooden bench, he couldn't help but grin, recalling how his partner, Doc, had employed every trick to upgrade their second-class passes to first-class. Doc, it seemed, had a penchant for luxury.

As Byron changed trains in Kansas City, his mind wandered to the bank manager who had carelessly directed Van de Velt and the others towards Abigail. He harboured a strong disdain for men who couldn't shut their mouths. Additionally, he pondered the money in the bank under Abigail's name. According to her will, it now belonged to him. While the sum wasn't substantial, Byron had instructed Abigail's lawyer to transfer it into his name. Not that he desired the money; it was a modest amount, but having those additional funds available for expenses while pursuing Van de Velt would be helpful. This, in addition to the nearly one thousand dollars he still had, would sustain him on the trail.

On the second day, Byron arrived in Chicago in the afternoon. Trains were remarkable, swift conveyances that covered vast distances efficiently. However, unlike riding a horse, you couldn't gaze down at the ground and read signs. The sensation of dismounting and feeling the soil underfoot was absent. Instead, the air carried the acrid scent of soot and cinders from the engine. Trains were fast and efficient, especially when urgency dictated, and Byron was indeed in a hurry.

As the train chugged into the Chicago yards, Byron retrieved his saddle and checked it at the luggage depot. He then went to a tavern he knew, not far from the station. His presence drew curious glances at a large man in weathered attire, carrying a bedroll and a substantial rifle, with a hefty revolver holstered at his side. Twenty years earlier, he might have blended into the background. Still, Chicago, as well as cities further west, had become increasingly refined and civilised. Anyone who didn't resemble a factory or office worker stood out conspicuously.

A burly man, clad in a shiny chequered suit and sporting a fuzzy vest straining over his ample belly, found amusement in Byron's passing. However, the laughter vanished abruptly when Byron met his gaze. Fearfully, the man offered a hasty acknowledgement and ushered the two ladies accompanying him down the street. Byron held little regard for cities. Occasionally, they served as convenient places to procure scarce necessities farther west. However, beyond that, their imposing structures and bustling streets felt confining. As he made his way towards his hotel, he sensed the weight of the buildings' rules, towering stories on either side of the narrow streets. The crowds of people jostling one another added to the sense of constriction—too many humans packed into too little space.

The scent enveloped Chicago, a city expanding alongside its human population, which swelled the ranks of animals: tens of thousands of horses, mules, and other livestock labouring for the citizens. Their presence transformed the streets into a malodorous quagmire. Jolting off the boardwalk into that muck was far from pleasant. Byron encountered no resistance, and within twenty minutes of disembarking the train, he checked into a modest hotel. The establishment lacked extravagance but was sufficiently clean, and he trusted that his belongings would remain undisturbed. After spending ten minutes washing off the grime from his railroad journey, he left the hotel. He made his way to the agency's offices.

As he ascended the office stairs, he intended to settle some old debts. Initially, those debts might go unpaid.

James Thomas informed Byron that they were dissatisfied with operatives pursuing personal vendettas. While they acknowledged his loss, they also recognised that operatives with excessive personal involvement in their cases tended to make numerous mistakes. Byron's resolve was unwavering.

"To hell with you," he declared. "I'll pursue them on my own." He strode towards the door, intent on his course of action.

However, James Thomas intervened with a call. "Hold on, Byron. Do not get on your high horse. While we don't typically endorse such methods, it's not out of the question. Given that you are the only individual who can identify Van de Velt and the others by sight, your approach may be our only viable option. Take a moment to consider my words."

Byron assured him that he would. He had achieved his goal: the US Marshals agency's total resources now stood firmly behind him. Once they had committed to a case, the establishment supported their men wholeheartedly; they were unyielding. Anyone who harmed a US Marshal operative would face severe consequences. Gardiner had always insisted that his men refer to themselves as US Marshals, not agents, sheriffs, or law enforcement officers.

Gardiner demanded excellence not only in technical skills but also in other aspects. Daily reports were mandatory, not only for the information they contained but also for learning regular habits. Marshals led mortal lives, except for the fraud required to achieve their goals, such as seducing a bandit's sister to extract vital information. All of this was in service of justice and was not considered moral turpitude by the indomitable Gardiner.

The agency meticulously sifted through the vast global gallery. Thousands of photographs passed through his fingers as he searched for any semblance of Boulder Ross and Dean Phillips. Each time a US Marshal apprehended a lawbreaker—whether dead or alive—they dutifully captured the man's likeness, photographing him before dispatching the image to the Chicago headquarters. These photographs were meticulously cross-indexed with the ceaseless stream of reports from field marshals and the agency's network of part-time, amateur informants.

Across the nation, a motley crew of contributors—bartenders, sheriffs, bankers, herders, and even cowboys—sent invaluable information. Some did so because they felt like they belonged to the United States Marshals agency. In contrast, the promise of substantial rewards enticed others. Although a wanted poster already existed for Daniel van de Velt, Byron still needed to uncover photographs of Ross or Phillips. However, he stumbled upon a modest file for each of these elusive men. The hunt was on.

Byron meticulously gathered all the available information about his quarry, Boulder Ross. He documented his usual haunts and patterns and comprehensively recorded his crimes. When Byron encountered Ross, the outlaw had been operating outside his typical territory. Ross, disliking cold weather, tended to wander the arid expanses of West Texas and New Mexico. In contrast, Dean Phillips felt right at home in the northern region.

Telegraphing word to informants across that region, a report arrived. A lively, stable owner in Montana confirmed that a man fitting Phillips's description had passed through just the day before, heading westward. Byron wasted no time. Within an hour, he was prepared to ride. Before departing, he swung by the office to establish communication lines with his colleagues. Byron didn't fuss over paperwork; he preferred sending reports more succinctly.

James Thomas reminded him to seek permission for any expenses exceeding fifty dollars. Byron nodded, muttering about skinflints. Fifty dollars didn't stretch far these days, but he was relieved to have his funds. James Thomas's parting words echoed as he stepped towards the door: "Send word if you find yourself in a tight spot." With a wry grin, Byron acknowledged the sentiment. The hunt was on, and he was ready to track down his prey.

15

MONTANA, THE FINAL FRONTIER

Phillips, seeking a strategic hiding spot, couldn't have chosen better. Montana, the final frontier, remained sparsely populated and challenging to access. Unfortunately for Byron, the usual swift route by train was unavailable, as the railroads hadn't yet extended into Montana. Curiously, the sole viable option was a journey via steamboat along the Missouri River, starting from St. Louis. This waterway would take him through Missouri, parts of Kansas, Nebraska, South and North Dakota, and the vast expanse of Montana, ultimately leading to Fort Creed. However, the river voyage was time-consuming, spanning several weeks. Moreover, during late summer, the rivers tended to run too shallow for efficient travel.

Faced with this obstacle, Byron retraced his steps, returning to the train to Cheyenne. His next leg of the journey involved horseback travel, necessitating the purchase of a suitable steed. To his surprise, quality horses were scarcer than he had anticipated. Byron regretted his oversight in Chicago and lamented not securing a sturdy steed to accompany him on his train journey. Fate intervened when he stumbled upon a robust yet ill-tempered horse that seemed to defy riders. Perhaps this equine possessed an intelligence that resisted human dominance, refusing to tolerate anyone on its back. Undeterred, Byron spent most of the day asserting his authority over the rebellious animal. In addition to his primary mount, Byron acquired a more modest companion, a second horse, to alternate with and give his main steed some much-needed rest. The combined cost of both animals exceeded one hundred dollars, which was a steep price in these remote, civilisation-fringed lands.

Avoiding contact with the Sheriff in Cheyenne, Byron grappled with conflicting emotions. On one hand, he sought to escape Mrs Van de Velt's reminders. On the other hand, he harboured possessive secrecy regarding Dean Phillips, considering him exclusively his own. As Byron embarked on the initial leg of his journey, the unforgiving terrain posed the most significant obstacle. The arid, barren land offered little respite. To ensure his horses' survival, he carried ample water, uncertain whether replenishment awaited him at day's end or after two or three days of riding.

As Byron rode through the rugged wilderness, phantom spectres materialised around him, stirred to life by the rhythmic pounding of hooves. His steeds bore the brunt of this arduous journey, and he frequently switched between them, carefully balancing the need for speed with their well-being. After days of relentless travel, Byron reached the North Fork of the Platte River. This wide watercourse, interrupted by sandbars, flowed swiftly even during this season, posing a formidable challenge. Undeterred, Byron veered westward, tracing the river's south bank for another day and a half until he discovered a suitable spot for fording.

Continuing his northward journey, Byron found himself in a less arid landscape. The following day, he crossed the Powder River and, two days later, the Tongue River. It was in the region between these two rivers that he encountered Native Americans for the first time. Byron bore some blame himself: he had failed to anticipate encountering hostiles this far south. Despite his assurance that the army's presence would keep the Cheyenne, Blackfoot, and Crow tribes occupied in the northern reaches of Montana, the harsh reality caught him off guard. The group he stumbled upon consisted of young warriors driven south by the allure of loot and glory. Riding atop a ridge without scouting the surroundings, Byron nearly stumbled into their midst. Approximately a dozen individuals, presumably Northern Cheyenne, dressed in war paint and most armed, confronted him. The Indians were startled, mirroring Byron's surprise.

Swiftly, he sprinted back to his horses, retracing his path. Within seconds, the pursuing Indians were hot on his heels, their arrows flying aimlessly. Although the Indians rode poorly, Byron managed to put distance between them. However, their relentless pursuit grated on him. He now headed in an unwanted direction; worse, his horses showed signs of fatigue. Byron, acutely aware of the Indians' dwindling mounts, suspected they would tenaciously follow his trail until either exhaustion or chance cornered him.

His desperate flight continued until he vanished from the sight of his pursuers. All the while, he scrutinised the rugged landscape around him. Finally, he spotted what he sought: a small hill that afforded a vantage point over his back trail for approximately a mile. He swiftly dismounted, secured his second horse's reins to the saddle horn, and looped the big bay's reins around his arm. Next, he retrieved his Winchester rifle and lay prone on the ground, poised and waiting. Minutes later, the Indians came into view, their formation slightly scattered as their horses faltered. However, there were eight of them, reasonably well grouped at the forefront. Byron adjusted his Winchester's rear sight, setting the crossbar for a range of approximately six hundred yards. He then engaged the set trigger, the faintest touch enough to ignite the rifle. With bated breath, he aimed down the long barrel, his heartbeat echoing in his ears. The leading warrior on his mount came into his sights, his finger exerting gentle pressure on the trigger. The rifle seemed to discharge of its own accord, the recoil slamming back against Byron's shoulder, propelling his body backwards.

The massive bullet hurtled towards the Indians, sealing his fate. As the lead rider's horse crashed heavily, flinging its rider over its head, the Indian lay stunned in the dust. Meanwhile, her comrade scrambled to his feet. Byron's centennial model, Winchester, had now proved its worth. Unlike most big-bore rifles, which were single-shot and capable of delivering a decisive blow at such a distance (like the Sharps), the Continental allowed Byron to lever round after round into the chamber, firing rapidly. Although he missed some shots, several horses went down before the Indians wisely retreated out of range. Yet one lone warrior persisted, either braver or foolhardier than the others. He charged wildly, clutching a long knife tightly in his right hand. Strangely, there was no sign of a firearm on him.

Byron's admiration for the man's courage was fleeting, overshadowed by a more pragmatic concern. He knew that killing any of the Indians would only escalate matters. The survivors would feel compelled to pursue him, seeking vengeance for their fallen companions. Therefore, he made a calculated decision: target the brave's horse rather than the brave himself. As the lone Cheyenne warrior closed in, Byron waited until he was within one hundred yards. With precise aim, he shot the horse out from beneath the rider. The Cheyenne, perhaps anticipating this move, executed a neat somersault and landed skilfully. Staggering a few steps past his fallen mount, he swiftly retrieved the spear he had dropped and charged forward on foot, still yipping wildly. Unfazed, Byron stood up, mounted his horse, and cantered away, leaving the cursing and shouting brave behind him.

The cost of losing valuable horses was steep, but he was willing to pay it to escape the relentless pursuit. Byron's desperate flight had forced the Indians to double up on their remaining horses, ultimately leading them to abandon the pursuit. He veered back towards the south bank of the Tongue River, albeit slightly west of his intended path, rolling in a wild circle.

The following day, he crossed into Montana, accompanied by two utterly exhausted horses. The Cheyenne chase, brief as it was, had pushed these animals to their limits. Dutifully, they plodded on, but the fire of resistance had vanished from the big bay. The second horse limped slightly, still moving forward but painfully slowly. Byron knew they would be helpful if he quickly cared for both animals. Now traversing immense rolling grasslands, Byron marvelled at Montana's reputed richness, ideal for grazing animals. These plains had once teemed with life: millions, tens of millions of creatures that sustained the Crow, Cheyenne, Sioux, Flatheads, and numerous other tribes. In the 1860s, buffalo coats became a fashion trend in the United States and Europe. However, this sartorial decision had a dark consequence: hide hunters descended upon the plains, mercilessly slaughtering millions of these massive, slow-moving creatures solely for their hides. The once-teeming buffalo herds were reduced to a haunting landscape of whitening bones, a grim testament to their decimation. The buffalo's plight persisted even after the buffalo coats fell out of favour. The army arrived, followed closely by settlers, and the hunters continued their relentless pursuit, this time for meat. The buffalo carcasses not only provided food for the military but also for the railroad workers further south and the captive Indians who were confined to barren reservations, their survival in peril. Byron faced a stark reality as he traversed the land: the once-thriving ecosystem had completely collapsed. Only a few antelope and scrawny coyotes remained—mere remnants of the countless animals that had roamed here just a decade earlier. Amid this desolation, the vast expanse of grasslands seemed like a perfect vacuum, beckoning the cattleman with its emptiness.

Father Desman, a Jesuit priest, drove one of Montana's earliest large cattle herds from Oregon to the Mission Valley in western Montana in the mid-1850s. After the Civil War, cattle drives from Texas brought significant stock to Montana. These herds arrived from various regions: some from Texas, others from California and Oregon, where abundant cattle posed challenges. Even herds from eastern Montana, originally intended to feed the men working the mountain mines, had outstripped the rugged western land's capacity to sustain them. Byron's encounter with his first herd occurred about a day's ride south of the Yellowstone River. Initially, he saw a massive cloud of dust approximately ten miles ahead. Determined, he urged his horses forward. After an hour, he arrived at the drag, where cowboys followed the herd to prevent any animals from falling behind or becoming lost. Dust covered their faces; bandannas shielded their lower faces from the grit, and these men engaged in the demanding task of riding drag. Although the average cowboy did not consider this role desirable, it fell to those with the least seniority. The dust-clad rider, his eyebrows caked in grit, finally spotted Byron. Urgently, he wheeled his horse to the nearest drag rider, about 200 yards away. That rider, in turn, relayed the message to the next, creating a chain of communication. Their cautious actions hinted at trouble during the drive, a common occurrence in this wild, untamed land. The idea that they hailed from Texas solidified; Montana was indeed a considerable distance from the Lone Star State.

"Howdy," the young rider greeted Byron. Despite his youth, he exuded toughness. Byron returned the greeting with equal warmth. "The boss man around?"

"Up near the front of the herd," the rider replied laconically. "Reckon if you ride up that way, you'll find him coming back."

Byron nodded, turned his mount, and ventured into the dust cloud. As the individual cattle materialised like small ships emerging from a dense sea fog, he noticed they were all longhorns, none of those fancy new eastern breeds. It was a massive herd of several thousand animals. Byron positioned himself on the windward side, halfway up one flank, free from the choking dust. Three men cantered toward him, the leader distinguished by his size and better attire. After miles of riding alongside this slow-moving cattle procession, he looked as prosperous as a man could under such circumstances. The trio halted their horses when they reached Byron, subtly fanning out into a cautious stance.

"Adam Cameron's the name," the big man declared. "What might you be doing out this way?"

Byron, bound for Helena out west, welcomed the prospect of company. His desire for a new horse, however, met a roadblock. Cameron candidly explained that their remuda was currently depleted. As for companionship, most of the boys would likely appreciate a fresh face.

"Why don't you ride up with us towards the point?" Cameron suggested.

Guided by Cameron, Byron followed the herd's trajectory. His horses struggled to keep pace with the others. Once they reached the dust-thickened vantage point out in front of the herd, Cameron offered, "Tell you what," he said. "You can turn your animals in with our remuda. Bordeaux and our nags will provide them with some respite. But be prepared to work a bit."

Byron accepted gratefully. A designated guide led him back to the remuda. These herds of horses were essential for trail outfits. Since all cattle driving work happened from horseback, a taxing endeavour, the ability to change mounts frequently was crucial, especially when the going got tough. When they reached the remuda, the man with

Byron instructed the head wrangler, a young boy probably no older than sixteen, to let him cut out a mount. Most horse wranglers were young and often lacked the experience required for the intricate riding and roping work of seasoned cowboys. Byron surveyed the fresh-looking animals, selected one, snubbed it to a bush, and transferred his saddle and gear from his tired mount. A young cowhand led his horses, who were then herded in with the rest of the remuda. Despite the big bays nearing exhaustion, it pranced alongside the other horses, head held high, searching for the head stallion—a challenge ready to unfold. Some horses snorted and shied, but being herd animals, Byron knew they were unlikely to bolt, especially with this much equine company. Byron returned to the point where he joined Cameron. The nod between them was followed by a silence that lingered for a few minutes.

Eventually, Cameron broke the silence. "What might be taking you out towards Helena? That's a fair piece down the road if there was a road."

"I'm fixing to meet a man there," Byron replied.

Cameron's next question was as direct as politeness allowed: "Are you a lawman?"

"More or less," Byron answered.

Cameron scrutinised him, and then Byron confirmed, "Marshall."

"Uh-huh."

Byron's sidelong glance at Cameron held a silent plea: keep this latest revelation to yourself. Cowboys and working people, in general, harboured little affection for the United States Marshal's agency. They associated it too closely with the bosses, the wealthy elite. Although this sentiment might be less pronounced among cowboys since they were too fiercely independent to let bosses push them around, it was a different story for miners. Miners had ample reasons to despise the agency. Too many of their own had fallen victim to United States Marshals during labour strikes. Byron's sympathies leaned toward the miners. The marshals they despised belonged to another faction of the agency, the protection side. These were the men hired out as guards and gunmen—individuals he had no use for. Cameron's disposition seemed inclined toward discretion. As they rode together, he gradually opened up. Weary from the trail, he was eager for conversation.

"We came up from down around San Antonio," he shared. "Nearly five months herding these stubborn lumps of meat." He gestured toward the plodding cattle, their dust-covered forms stretching into the distance. "My range was nearly depleted, and I heard about the grass up this way from others who'd ventured here and liked it. So here I am, cattle, gear, and all. And I'll tell you, so far, I like the look of this grass. The cattle are already regaining some of the weight they lost along the trail."

Byron engaged in polite chatter, mindful that he was riding Cameron's horse. Yet his thoughts remained fixed on Philips, still several days' ride to the west if Philips was indeed there and not a mere phantom. Despite his yearning to head westward, he recognised the necessity of spending a few days with the herd, allowing his horses to recuperate. That night, Byron savoured his first full meal in days, sitting around the fire with his hands. A big chipped enamel bowl of beef stew lay before him. The cowboys, especially the younger ones, regarded him with a hint of shyness. He was of a different breed. The way he wore his .44, the deer he had bagged, and the intensity in his eyes signalled that he made his living vastly differently. Yet, they were as friendly as poppies, and Byron found himself warming to them. Their lives seemed far less complicated than his—no Dean Phillips, Boulder Ross, or Mrs. Van de Velt. That night, he slept close to the fire. For the first time in ages, he didn't tether himself to his horses with reins looped around his wrist. He dared not merely doze; his senses remained alert for danger. The soft, soothing singing of the night herd drifted in from the cattle. Just before sleep claimed him, he wondered what it would be like to lead a straightforward life of freedom and honest, hard work—a life spent in the saddle alongside each cowboy. He felt like the lord of creation, perched so high, miles above the poor souls toiling on or beneath the ground. Yet even as he entertained this notion, he recognised that such a life could not endure much longer. He had witnessed the relentless spread of endless miles of fencing across thousands of square miles that had once been open range. If they persisted in their cowboy ways, these same cowboys would eventually have to dismount and dig holes for fence posts. They would need to cultivate and harvest winter fodder. Once those fences encircled the land, it would be the sole means of feeding their confined herds. For now, Byron found solace lying by the fire. The soft crooning of nighthawks and the good-natured banter of drowsy cowboys enveloped him. The earth's scent rose from beneath him, and he could let down his guard against the morning for these precious days.

Byron remained with Cameron's herd until they reached the Yellowstone River. Still astride Cameron's horses, he assisted in moving the cattle across. The Yellowstone, broad and relatively deep, necessitated swimming the animals—both horses and cattle—across its expanse. Fortunately, the crossing proceeded smoothly, with only a cow or two lost. Cameron shared that they had faced floods in Nebraska after a storm, losing about three hundred heads. Tragically, a man drowned when his horse rolled over during a river crossing. On the third day, Byron parted ways with the herd and once again mounted his own horse. The animals were in better shape now, especially the bay. The other horse, which he led most of the time, was strong for the moment but lacked the endurance of the bay. Byron's path led west toward the western Montana Mountains, the initial settling region. Two decades earlier, as the California Gold Fields waned, miners had pushed eastward over the hills in search of more gold. Their quest led them to south-western Montana, where towns like Bannock and Virginia City sprang up—rough, bustling settlements teeming with desperate miners and the parasites that preyed upon their labour: gamblers, whores, and bandits. Byron had heard tales of those early days, the wild, lawless times when Montana was still a raw frontier. Law enforcement was scarce, and one notorious band of outlaws, improbably named the "Defenders," wreaked havoc. Under the leadership of a man named Harry McCall, they robbed and killed with impunity. But the tide turned when vigilant citizens organised an efficient group of vigilantes. Many men, including McCall, met their fate at the end of a hangman's noose. As the area settled, the rugged Montana landscape remained challenging. It was a natural refuge for men like Dean Phillips. The further west Byron travelled, the more treacherous the terrain became. Steep, forested mountains loomed, their spiny peaks accentuated by tall, slender conifers. In some places, the hills were stripped bare, trees felled to feed the insatiable hunger of mines, stamp mills, and towns for firewood. Approaching the mining areas, the land bore the scars of relentless exploitation. Near Helena, Byron found himself surrounded by gutted valleys and hillsides. Hydraulic hoses had washed away soil in the frantic search for gold, leaving behind massive piles of mine tailings. The mountains themselves had been hollowed out, their interiors ripped apart. Civilization beckoned once more, the abode of men. When Byron arrived in Helena, he made a beeline for the livery stable that had sent the wire regarding Dean Phillips. The stable owner, who had dispatched the message, appeared astute enough to identify the man accurately. Although there remained a slim chance of error—a look-alike perhaps—the stable owner was adamant. He vividly recalled that particular individual; he had damaged a horse from the stable and even threatened to gut the stable owner when confronted. The behaviour certainly aligned with Phillips's reputation. Word had it that Phillips was en route to Mallard. There, gambling opportunities abounded. Some enthusiasts were even discussing the development of a seemingly worthless copper deposit into a substantial copper mine, the Charlton Mine. Reports mentioned millions invested in mills, poles, buildings, and plans to introduce a railroad. The allure of money hung in the air, drawing men like Phillips. Byron's journey led him to Mallard, an unattractive collection of shanty houses and mine pits. In the local saloons, he gathered information that a man resembling Phillips had passed through, heading south toward the old, depleted goldfields near Charlton. As Byron continued, the land grew rougher and bleaker. The area showed scant signs of human habitation, with scattered cabins dotting the landscape. Most nights, he slept out on the trail, securing the big bay's reins around his wrist. One night, however, the animals' restlessness alarmed him. Byron lay motionless, senses alert. It took fifteen minutes to realise that his spare horse, hobbled some forty yards away, was missing. With morning light, he set out to track the horse. Someone was riding it, and despite its recent limp, Byron knew he could catch up to whoever had taken it.

Byron faced a group of six Flathead Indians huddled in a slight depression. Among them were an older man, two scrawny children of about eight years old, a young woman, and a skeletal old crone whose survival seemed miraculous. Their wretched thinness revealed their desperate state—they were starving. This desperation had driven them to steal the horse. The older man, a seasoned warrior, must have orchestrated the theft. With the buffalo gone and their people confined to reservations, suffering under corrupt Indian agents who pilfered meagre government food rations, the older man had no alternative but to forage. Byron's horse was nearby. The saddlebags had already been removed, and the women were butchering the animal. Strips of meat sizzled over a small fire. Perched on the skyline, Byron observed the group below. He detected no signs of firearms among them. The older man spotted him first.

Despair etched the warrior's features shortly, but then he reached for a knife and began chanting a death chant, perhaps as he climbed the hill toward Byron. Byron watched the older man's determined ascent. Despite his evident weakness from hunger, the warrior pressed on. He slipped once, rolling partway back down the hill. Acting swiftly, Byron dismounted and offered some bacon and a couple of cans of beans from his saddlebags, tossing them down the hill—it was all the food he had. The cans rolled past the older man, who stared at them uncomprehendingly. Byron raised his hand again in a peace sign, then turned his horse and rode away.

Arriving in the Charlton area, Byron's mood soured. The degradation and pain weighed on him nearly as much as Abigail's death. The image of the older woman and the starving children haunted him. As he continued, he passed isolated homesteads. In such remote regions, local gossip served as a vital source of information for an operative. Even in this rugged area, Dean Phillips stood out as an evil little bastard. By the time Byron reached town, he knew he would find Phillips there. He recalled which saloon Phillips frequented, aware that time was running out for Dean Phillips.

16

RECOGNITION DAWNED

Phillips, a man of dubious reputation, frequented a dingy little saloon that perfectly mirrored the seedy town where he had taken refuge. Byron, however, didn't rush in recklessly. He had no desire for a swift confrontation. Instead, he conducted stealthy reconnaissance, riding through town in the darkness, ensuring he remained hidden in the shadows. The saloon emitted a feeble glow from its half-open door, leaving Byron to wonder if Phillips lurked inside. Patience was his ally. Byron set up camp approximately five miles away, nestling amidst dense brush, confident that no one would detect him. He refrained from returning to town until the following night. Disembarking from his horse, he covered the last hundred yards on foot, leaving the steed tethered to a tree beyond the farthest building. Byron positioned himself alongside the saloon's wall, where a single, grimy window provided a glimpse into the interior. Voices emanated from within, and he pressed his face against the glass, peering into the murky depths of the establishment. He prepared for the inevitable encounter with Phillips.

Inside the saloon, the seediness intensified. A scarred and sagging bar stretched along one wall, its history etched into the wood. Faded pictures adorned the walls, hanging crookedly in a chaotic display. The floor bore the weight of old furniture, creating a cluttered maze. Amidst this disarray, a massive, slightly sway-backed pool table dominated what little unoccupied space remained. Two inebriated patrons huddled over the ripped, stained green cloth covering the pool table. Their bent cues ineffectually prodded at chipped balls, creating a clumsy spectacle. Meanwhile, Dean Phillips held court on the opposite side of the room. Leaning against the bar, he cradled a glass of whisky, lazily observing the drunks' eight-ball game. Byron's gaze bore into Phillips. The man seemed disturbingly at ease, which grated on Byron's nerves. This equilibrium needed disruption. Unseen, Byron lingered by the window, the dim light filtering through the grime-covered pane and casting him as a mere shadow. He urged Phillips to glance his way. Eventually, Phillips did. His eyes swept lazily over the glass, and then he moved on, only to snap back. Recognition dawned, and tension ripped through his body. He spun and bolted towards the door without hesitation, leaving the saloon in a flurry of urgency. The game had begun. Byron swiftly vanished in the cloak of darkness, melding into the shadows. He sought refuge behind a stack of crates just seconds before Phillips emerged, striding briskly around the building's corner. The obscurity halted Phillips in his tracks, and he squinted into the night, suspicion etching his features.

"Who the hell is out there?" he demanded.

Byron held his breath, remaining utterly still. He doubted Phillips would venture into the unknown. Approaching an unseen adversary in the transition from light to darkness was reckless, even for someone as unhinged as Phillips. Phillips retraced his steps as if sensing his vulnerability, disappearing around the corner. A moment later, the rusty hinges of the saloon door creaked. Evidently, Phillips had feigned retreat, but Byron maintained his motionless vigil. After a brief interlude, Phillips's head reappeared, cautiously peering into the shadows. His retreat had been a ruse—a calculated ploy to lure out his adversary. The game continued, each move fraught with tension. Byron maintained his position for several minutes, then nonchalantly shrugged and pivoted, vanishing from view. As the door hinges squealed again, he was confident that Phillips had retreated into the saloon. Swiftly, Byron moved towards his horse. The calculated plan was to leave Phillips questioning his senses—had it been mere imagination conjuring ghostly images in empty windows? Byron, a man well-versed in shadows and secrets, would play the role of the enigmatic phantom.

For another day, Byron remained in the shadows. His reconnaissance had borne fruit: Phillips's sleeping quarters lay a quarter of a mile beyond town, nestled in a modest cabin. While Phillips caroused in the saloon one afternoon, Byron seized the opportunity. The cabin's door lacked a lock, granting easy access. The shabby interior revealed traces of Dickensian hardship for a man who had once ridden with one of the West's most successful robber gangs. Yet Phillips's inability to hold onto money was evident. The single room, scarcely deserving the term "furnished," harboured a broken-down bed in one corner. A three-legged stool lay abandoned near the bed, and the chipped washbasin appeared to have forgotten its recent use.

Byron set the stage for the final act. Byron, ever the strategist, had prepared meticulously. Unfurling a large piece of cloth, he laid it on the bed in the dimly lit cabin. The bloodstains, stark against the torn and shredded fabric, bore witness to the grim history of what remained of Abigail's dress. Byron trained his binoculars on the cabin from a safe distance, observing every move. As Phillips entered, the air thickened with anticipation. For several heartbeats, silence reigned. Then a cry pierced the night, and Phillips burst out of the door. In one hand, he clutched the torn dress; in the other, a pistol. His wild gaze swept the surroundings.

"What the hell is going on?" he shouted, his pistol's barrel oscillating between directions. "Goddamn it!" he screamed. "If you're out there, step into the open and face me like a grown-up!"

Their fateful confrontation was about to unfold. The silence hung heavy, refusing to yield any answers. Perhaps sensing his vulnerability amidst the vast empty land, Phillips retreated into the cabin. Byron, ever the shadow, slipped away soundlessly. How long would Phillips remain holed up, grappling with the enigma that enveloped him? Undoubtedly, suspicion would gnaw at Byron's presence, like a phantom haunting the edges of his consciousness. Who else could have laid hands on that dress? The days stretched on, and as Byron failed to reappear, perhaps the little bastard's mind played tricks on him. Did Abigail rise from the grave? Phillips, teetering on the edge of sanity, was no stranger to madness. Yet his brand of insanity was immune to guilt; it lacked conscience altogether. The next time Byron glimpsed him, Phillips moved about as if nothing had transpired. The game continued with each step, a precarious dance on the cusp of fate. Byron, the shadowed avenger, perched on a ridge overlooking

Phillips' cabin with unyielding resolve. Aware that Phillips typically returned late from the saloon, Byron bided his time. As the sun climbed towards its zenith, subtle movements within the cabin caught his attention. Around noon, Phillips emerged shirtless and bootless towards the outhouse. Byron allowed him to approach within ten yards before unleashing a calculated barrage from his Winchester. The bullets, purposefully aimed wide, churned up clouds of dirt around Phillips. The man staggered, momentarily disoriented, his shoulders jerking in response. He was only half-awake, yet instinct propelled him to sprint to cover in the house's safety. Byron persisted; each shot was a deliberate warning. The bullets danced perilously close to Phillips's bare feet, urging him onward.

Desperation fuelled his dive through the door, seeking refuge within. However, Byron wasn't done. He continued to burn, shattering the single window, shredding the door, and demolishing the rickety stovepipe. Satisfied, he descended the ridge, retracing his steps towards his horse. As he rode away, the faint pop of Phillips's pistol echoed, interwoven with hoarse curses. What was Phillips shooting at? Ghosts, perhaps? A wry smile tugged at Byron's lips as he envisioned Phillips frantically burrowing through the splintered floor. At the same time, those hefty .45-calibre bullets wreaked havoc on the cabin. Perhaps, just maybe, Phillips had finally met his opponent.

Phillips's abrupt departure marked the beginning of a relentless pursuit. Concealed atop a hill, Byron watched Phillips spurring his mount onto the trail. Byron exercised patience, rolling into town, replenishing supplies, and then resuming his position along the same path. Phillips's trail was initially conspicuous; he made no effort to conceal his tracks. Byron followed leisurely, but his instincts and training soon signalled a shift. Swerving off the main trail, he ascended to higher ground. Two hours later, Byron detected Phillips's ambush. The man had ensconced himself on a slight rise, peering down the trail behind a clump of brush. The tell-tale glint of a rifle muzzle betrayed his intent. Byron positioned himself behind trees, mirroring his earlier tactic. Bullets rained around Phillips, who, hampered by the limited range of his weapon, had no recourse but to flee, zigzagging down the trail. Byron relentlessly pursued Phillips for three more days, pushing him to the brink of madness. Now, he allowed Phillips a glimpse of his presence, appearing briefly on the skyline, perhaps only two or three hundred yards away, before vanishing beyond reach. Phillips lacked the wilderness experience to retaliate effectively. He was a barroom brute who relied on viciousness to intimidate others. But out here, in the unforgiving wild, his brutality yielded nothing. Byron relentlessly pursued Phillips, challenging him with sheer mountains with crumbling slopes, sparsely wooded by the same spiny conifers found further north. Water was scarce, and Byron suspected that Phillips, who lacked the skill to locate water sources, was growing increasingly thirsty. Desperation drove Phillips. Concealed half a mile away, Byron observed Phillips guiding his horse onto rocky ground, attempting to obscure his trail. Byron allowed him to believe he had successfully evaded pursuit. Byron remained cautious over the next three days, ensuring Phillips never caught sight of him. He could sense when Phillips thought he had shaken off his pursuer. Despite fatigue weighing heavily on him, Phillips rode more confidently, glancing back less frequently.

On the third night, utterly worn out, Phillips made camp beside a small, swiftly flowing stream. He retired late, well past midnight, likely assuming the cover of darkness would conceal his location even if someone trailed him. The quarter moon and starlight, aided by the potency of Byron's field glasses, kept Phillips within sight. While approaching on foot might provide greater security, Byron refrained from risking a fire. The stakes were high, and the game of cat and mouse continued under the watchful celestial canopy.

However, Byron had gambled on something even more formidable: the swift, babbling stream. Its raucous noise drowned out most other sounds. Byron observed Phillips unfurl his bedroll from his concealed vantage point, settle into it, and surrender to sleep. For hours, Byron remained vigilant, ensuring Phillips's slumber was deep and unbroken. Then, under the cover of dawn, he embarked on his final approach, moving silently on foot. The stream's clamour masked Byron's footsteps. He advanced cautiously, inch by inch. Within an hour, he closed the gap to ten yards from his slumbering quarry. Another half-hour of watchful waiting ensued. As the eastern sky began to lighten, revealing more details, Byron noticed Phillips's rifle propped against a nearby tree, barely a yard from his head. The pistol lay outside the bedroll, still holstered. It was inches from Phillips's right hand, but it should have been inside the bedroll; Byron would have played it that way. Methodically, Byron shifted the pistol and rifle out of reach. Phillips's knife remained elusive, but that was typical. It likely lay concealed within the bedroll. No matter. With the firearms neutralised, Byron stood tall and walked to a rock roughly ten yards from Phillips. He then settled down, facing the slumbering man. Phillips, accustomed to late mornings and utterly exhausted, showed no signs of stirring, even as full daylight bathed the landscape. The sun would rise in another fifteen minutes, illuminating the final act of their deadly dance. Byron's calculated moves had led him to this decisive moment.

As small pebbles danced towards Phillips, the man grunted, swatting at invisible pests with closed eyes. A pebble grazed his cheek, and his eyelids fluttered open, scanning the campsite. Recognition dawned as he locked eyes with Byron.

"Morning, Dean," Byron greeted, his tone deceptively pleasant. "You're definitely one for sleeping."

Phillips's hand darted for his pistol, but Byron pre-empted him, brandishing Phillips's gun belt. "Looking for something?" he asked. He hurled the belt into the brush, and the rifle followed suit. Phillips attempted to rise, but Byron now held his pistol, the hammer's click audible even above the stream's cacophony. Phillips froze, caught in fate's crosshairs.

"About time we had a little talk," Byron declared, raising his voice to carry over the rushing water. Phillips remained motionless, his mind racing. Why hadn't Byron pulled the trigger already? When would the shot come? But if Byron chose to delay the inevitable with conversation, Phillips would play along for now. The wilderness held its breath, awaiting the outcome of their deadly dance. Byron, his resolve unyielding, confronted Phillips in the wilderness in a deadly dance of vengeance and survival. The sun hung low, casting elongated shadows across the rugged terrain.

"I'm surprised to see you're doing so poorly," Byron remarked, his voice deceptively calm. "I figured you had it all figured out that Van de Velt would make you a rich man."

"Van de Velt?" Phillips echoed.

"Yeah, the boss. That son of a bitch!" His anger flared. "He only gave me a couple of thousand bucks. Then, one night, when I was drunk, he and Ross took off with the rest of the loot."

Byron's smile was intimidating. "That's their last resort, isn't it? However, we both know you will not see them again, Dean. Because it's you who's the dead man."

Phillips flinched as Byron raised the pistol, but his hands dipped inside the bedroll. Byron anticipated the inevitable. Yet, in an unexpected twist, Byron lowered his .44 and set it aside. Phillips remained frozen. Standing, Byron reached behind his belt, withdrawing his massive bowie knife.

"Time to finish it, Dean," he murmured. Joyful incredulity flickered across Phillips's face. In an instant, he sprang from the bedroll, wicked blade in hand.

"You stupid sucker!" Phillips sniggered, bouncing on the balls of his feet. "You're the one who is a dead man!"

Byron retorted. The two men squared off. Byron anchored himself, holding loosely the hefty bowie in front of him. Phillips resembled a panther more than a man; he was agile, fluid, and deadly. His knife lunged towards Byron's stomach, but it was a feint. Byron shifted, the blade grazing past him. The dance intensified, and each move was a calculated gamble. The wilderness held its breath, waiting for the final strike to push his advantage and hurt Byron more, but he was enjoying himself too much to rush things.

"So... you figured you had to play it fair," he smirked. "You had to do it this way; give me an even chance. Well, you big stupid lump of dog shit, it's not even at all because I'm going to cut you up into little strips and give you to the nearest Indian to dry into jerky meat."

Byron said nothing. He remained standing solidly, a thin trickle of blood running down his left arm, his knife steady in front of his body. He let Phillips prance around some more, and then he suddenly moved forward more quickly than such a big man should have been able to move. While Phillips was preoccupied with his conversation, Byron's heavy blade unexpectedly struck his lighter on one side, and the ball's broad tip sliced through his shirt, creating a shallow groove across his chest.

"Son of a bitch!" Phillips cursed, dodging away, his knife slashing the air close to Raider's eyes, forcing him to halt his advance. The play was over, and the fight was on in earnest, but neither man could seem to break through the other's guard. So Phillips began to taunt his opponent, hoping to make him angry and trick him into losing control. He taunted him with the one thing that would hurt him most—Abigail's death. Phillips's twisted grin revealed a dark truth.

"She was one hell of a fighter," he admitted. "I kept kicking and squirming even after it was in her." His words hung heavy, and he clarified, "And I wasn't talking about my knife, though that found its way later, too."

"Damn. I never thought a woman could have so much blood in her," Phillips added. The wilderness bore witness to their brutal dance, one that would leave scars etched in memory long after the screams had faded. Byron's face remained stoic as Phillips closed in, desperate for words. However, Byron sprang into action once more. Phillips, too near, staggered back, his left hand flailing for balance. In a swift, complex arc, Byron's bowie sliced through all four fingers of Phillips's left hand, just behind the second knuckle. Phillips staggered away, out of reach, staring at the white bone and pink flesh. The razor-sharp blade left clean stumps, blood seeping into Phillips's palm as he gazed at the remnants of his hand.

Now, it was Phillips who lost control. He had never suffered such severe cuts in a knife fight before. "You sack of sh*t!" he screamed, lunging forward and slashing wildly. Byron, surgical in his precision, opened deep, long cuts on Phillips's arms, thighs, and forehead. Blood streamed into Phillips's eyes, blinding him. The dance of death continued, with each move marking their fates in the wilderness. Knowing that he was in great danger and that loss of blood would soon weaken him so much that he wouldn't be able to defend himself, Phillips put the last of his energy into one final attack, lunging forward, his blade drawing blood again, this time from Byron's knife arm, a shallow cut, and then he drew in deep, aiming the long, slender tip of his blade upwards, at a point just below Byron's sternum, though Byron blocked the thrust with a bowie, forcing Phillips's knife arm back. Then he seized it with his left hand, freeing him to move inside. With great power, he drove forward, sinking most of his fifteen inches of Bowie knife deep into Phillips's belly. Phillips shuddered from the shock, eyes wide in amazement; he was aware of the entire blade still inside his body. The two men stood toe to toe for a few seconds, with Phillips shuddering from head to foot. Byron suddenly twisted the knife and ripped it sideways, hard, opening a mass of the wound in Phillips's abdomen. Phillips did not cry out until the knife had left his body, and then he screamed a high, thin sound. He slowly bent forward, trying to hold in his cuts as they spewed from his body. He knelt on the ground, his hands laden with intestinal contents, a significant portion of which twisted his face. Byron stood back, watching his enemy as he knelt, before he muttered,

"It doesn't feel good when it's happening to you, does it?"

Phillips remained on his knees, seemingly afraid to move. Byron walked over, picked up his pistol, and holstered it. He took one last look at Phillips, then strolled into the trees, heading towards his horse. He had only gone about halfway when the first agonised screams echoed from the campsite. Byron kept walking, reached his horse, and swung into the saddle. The screams intensified. He guided his horse towards the trail, the wails trailing behind him. Even after riding about half a mile, the screams persisted. Byron halted his horse, sitting motionless in the saddle. The sound now grew more guttural and faded slightly. Abruptly, he wheeled his horse around and galloped back towards the clearing.

Dean Phillips still knelt when Byron reached him, but his hands now rested at his sides, his intestines trailing into the ground before him. As Byron rode closer, hope flickered in Phillips's eyes.

"Please," he muttered, his voice barely recognisable. "Hurts... so much..."

Byron shot him between the eyes. The two hundred and fifty grain bullet slammed Phillips onto his back, his legs still folded beneath him. His body twitched several times and then lay still. Byron set the hammer on half-cock, opened the loading gate, and ejected the empty shell casing. After one last glance at the remnants of Dean Phillips, he chambered a fresh round, holstered the pistol, spun his mount, and rode away. As he rode, he wondered why he didn't feel any better, why this act hadn't brought Abigail back to him.

17

THE VENDETTA WEIGHED HEAVILY ON HIM

Byron's relentless pursuit of Dean Phillips had led him almost to the Utah border. We headed south, with Salt Lake City just a day's ride away. The terrain here was gentler, in contrast to the harsh area where Phillips lay dead, his remains scavenged by animals.

Upon reaching Salt Lake City, Byron sent a telegram to the Chicago office. He reported Dean Phillips' demise and requested information about Daniel van de Velt's whereabouts. The agency's response arrived two days later, revealing that Boulder Ross was again up to his old tricks, probing banks, express offices, and any other places with a hint of wealth—this time in West Texas.

Without hesitation, Byron sold his sturdy bay horse at a livery stable for twenty dollars below its current value. The seasoned trail-man in him considered buying another horse and perhaps a pack animal to head south immediately. The allure of the Canyon Country in Southeast Utah—a desolate yet strikingly sculpted land of sandstone and shale—beckoned. Beyond that lay the Taos area in New Mexico, which was equally tempting. But there was no time for leisure. Byron needed to catch up with Boulder Ross and Daniel van de Velt, and they would pay for their deeds.

Yet Abigail's voice persisted, a spectral echo in Byron's mind. Like fragile threads, her words wove through his thoughts, urging him to release the burden of vengeance and reclaim his own life. The vendetta weighed heavily on him, threatening to consume all that remained of his existence.

On that afternoon train, bound for Cheyenne once more, Byron pondered the strange alignment of fate. Why did the pursuit of Daniel van de Velt and his gang repeatedly lead him through Cheyenne? It could be destiny or mere happenstance. Regardless, the rail line to Cheyenne offered the swiftest route around the colossal obstacle of the Rocky Mountains.

From Cheyenne, he boarded another train, this time bound for Denver. The journey was a brief day's passage. The flat plains stretched endlessly to the east, while the rugged mountains stood sentinel in the west, their imposing peaks forming a jagged barrier known as the Front Range. Denver lay beneath this natural fortress, a city on the brink of possibility.

Byron hesitated. Should he seek out Gardiner at the Denver office? Time was precious, and the telegram from Chicago had already revealed what he needed to know: the remaining two men he hunted might lurk to the south in the vast expanse of West Texas. The pursuit continued, fuelled by determination and haunted by Abigail's whispered entreaties.

In late September, I painted the Colorado mountains with a vibrant palette. Aspens and cottonwoods, adorned in their seasonal plumage, created a vivid splash of colour against the dark green of the conifers. Byron was tempted to pause and rest, but he knew he could not prolong the risk of someone else reaching Ross before he did.

As the rails climbed higher into the mountains, they abruptly halted. For years, the Santa Fe Railroad had clashed with the Denver and Rio Grande Railroads over the right of way into New Mexico. These rival companies hired gunmen to harass each other's work camps, creating a volatile atmosphere. Meanwhile, the ongoing feud caused a delay in the train's progress.

From the railhead, Byron embarked on a stagecoach journey to Santa Fe. This little pueblo's high, dry plateau had changed little since its Spanish founding over two centuries ago. Flat-roofed, whitewashed buildings stood resolute under the brilliant Mexican sun, seamlessly blending with the dun-coloured landscape. Wherever water flowed, aspens and cottonwoods thrived. The air, crisp and pure, matched Byron's preference for clarity. The population in this place was a fascinating blend of Spanish, Pueblo Indians, and a sprinkling of Anglos. The air carried a sense of tranquillity.

Despite days without rest, Byron secured a room in a modest hotel. His hunger led him to devour a meal heavily seasoned with chilli peppers. As he retired to his room in the late afternoon, the fiery aftermath left him belching. The lingering heat clung to the space, and he settled onto the narrow cot, the room's primary piece of furniture. Above him, dark, weathered beams stretched across the whitewashed ceiling. A guitar strummed softly somewhere nearby, and the distant murmur of Spanish floated through the window. The ambience held an ageless quality. Yet the urge to halt and cease his relentless pursuit teased him again—only briefly.

As he drifted asleep, Byron made a silent vow: he would not yield. He would press forward, driven by the need to avenge Abigail.

The previous day, he had acquired a magnificent black stallion for fifty dollars. Now, at the livery stable, he saddled up an hour before dawn. As the first light peeked over the eastern horizon, the sky transformed into a marvellous shade of light mauve. In these arid lands, dawn unfolded swiftly, and the sun blazed forth with astonishing purity, etching its brilliance against the distant horizon. Byron rode out of town, resolute and unwavering.

Byron's journey unfolded south-eastward, with the morning sun casting a glow over his left shoulder. The trail descended from the lofty heights, leading him out of the rugged terrain. Within a day and a half, he found himself in the scorching expanse of New Mexico's arid desert, which bore the imprint of relentless sun and sparse vegetation.

Before departing Santa Fe, he'd received a stern warning: "Watch out for the Apaches. Nahche, Cochise's son, and a young warrior named Geronimo are on the prowl—the most severe outbreak of Indian unrest in the territory since Cochise's own time."

Despite his caution, Byron encountered no living Apaches. Yet, one late afternoon, a distant smudge of smoke caught his attention. He veered towards it, riding in an oblique circle until his field glasses revealed the smouldering remnants of a cabin about half a mile away. He approached cautiously, only to find the jagged wall stumps. The bodies of a white man, a woman, and a little girl lay together behind a low rock barrier. Brass cartridge cases littered the ground around them. There were no signs of torture. Instead, Byron pieced together a grim scenario: the man, desperate and with dwindling options, had likely shot both his wife and daughter before turning the gun on himself—understandably so, given what awaited them if the Apaches had taken them alive, especially the women.

The scalped bodies bore witness to the brutal reality of Apache warfare. Byron's grim task led him to a modest shed behind the house, its contents ravaged by looters. Among the few remnants, he found a shovel, its handle broken but still functional for his purpose. Lately, he had become all too familiar with digging graves. In sober silence, he placed the man in one shallow grave, and the woman and the little girl in another.

A distant snarl echoed from the brush as he began filling the earth. Curiosity drew him towards the sound, which revealed the lifeless body of an Apache warrior lying about forty yards from the ruined cabin. The deceased settler had managed to wound at least one of his attackers before succumbing. Four coyotes squabbled over the deceased Apache. Byron hesitated, leaning on the shovel and contemplating digging another hole. Ultimately, he shrugged off the impulse and returned to the graves, leaving the dead man to the scavengers. His aversion to Apaches ran deep; he had witnessed too much of their brutality.

Byron's destination lay in the lonely heart of West Texas, a sparsely populated and utterly barren expanse a day's ride west of Pecos. The monotonous landscape stretched out before him, featureless and unyielding. Finally, in a sad little town on the edge of nowhere, he found what he was looking for: the posse hunting Boulder Ross. Led by the formidable Sheriff Thomas H. Hoffin, the group eyed Byron warily. His status as a U.S. Marshal operative might make him a rival for the reward money. Byron wasted no time, laying his cards on the table. He knew there was no chance of pulling off the same trick he had managed with that Kansas sheriff. The stakes were higher now, and the pursuit was relentless. The Mitchell brothers' reward? You wouldn't dare try that manoeuvre with someone like Sheriff Thomas H. Hoffin.

Hoffin recounted Boulder Ross's most recent escapade. Ross and his gang had robbed a bank not too far from here. "It was a wild affair," he said, "bullets flying, people scrambling for cover, and plenty of hollering. But the haul? A meagre five hundred dollars at most. It didn't bother me much, though. We'll hang them as high as possible, whether it's five hundred or five thousand." Byron pressed, seeking confirmation: "You're sure it was Ross?" "Yeah, we caught one of them. He revealed that Ross was the leader of the group. That bandit blabbed about many things before he met his unfortunate end."

"Accident?" Byron asked.

The sheriff's mouth twitched—the closest thing to a grin Byron would witness during their acquaintance. "Yep, an accident. Sincerely, clumsy Ross fell from a box he was standing on, and the rope around his neck completed the deed. Any man who robs banks in my territory has to be. Nope, it was just Boulder Ross and his ragtag crew. Many misfits are likelier to shoot off their toes than execute a clean bank robbery." Byron had already suspected as much. If Van de Velt had orchestrated the heist, it would have unfolded far more smoothly. A lingering hope that it could all end right here fuelled his inquiry.

Ross's gang had left an unmistakable trail. A dozen determined men, led by the sheriff, prepared to pursue them. When Byron asked to join, Hoffin didn't object.

"Why not?" he replied, a hint of struggle in his voice. "You marshals can witness firsthand how we Texans deal with the bad apples."

They set out without delay. Byron doubted he had ever ridden alongside a tougher-looking bunch, even more formidable than the boss's gang. They rode relentlessly, slashing the distance between themselves and the outlaws. The bandits' trail pointed westward.

"They're probably trying to make it to El Paso, then down into Mexico and the easy life," Hoffin said laconically. "I wired ahead. They won't be able to get through that way."

The next day, the posse reached the tiny settlement of Sawn Hill. The landscape had transformed into low, barren hills. Yet, these hills held a certain charm, especially after the monotony of the endless, desolate plain. Adobe houses made up the majority of Sawn Hill, with a few frame structures constructed by wealthy Anglos. A posse riding east had clashed with Ross's gang. Four of the bandits lay dead, reducing their numbers to six or seven. The survivors had ridden off in haste, heading towards the border, a mere twenty or thirty miles away.

"Okay, boys, let's push it hard," Hoffin curtly instructed his men.

The bandits' trail now led south through the mountains. This terrain was far more challenging—rugged expanse with plenty of ground to cover. Water was scarce, forcing each man to ration what he had. The heat was unrelenting, like an eternal sheet in southern Texas. The broken ground made tracking the fleeing bandits a formidable task, but Byron's keen eye picked up traces when no one else could. Hoffin never acknowledged it openly, but Byron sensed his silent approval.

As the sun dipped towards the horizon, they spotted seven bandits riding weary horses about a mile ahead.

The chase commenced, with the posse urging their mounts, their weariness shortly forgotten. The bandits, aware of their pursuers, strained to escape, but the gap between the two groups gradually closed. As twilight settled in, it narrowed to gunshot range. The bandits fought back, knowing that capture meant certain death. One by one, they fell, shot out of their saddles, until darkness obscured their targets. Only two remained— the ones with the best horses. They vanished into the night. Byron was certain that Boulder Ross was among them.

"Let's hold up here, boys," Sheriff Hoffin signalled.

Byron could not fathom the delay. The fleeing men were mere hundreds of yards away. Even in the dark, the posse could fan out and box them in. Byron's impatience grew; he knew one of those fleeing figures was Boulder Ross.

"I believe that Mexico is just a short distance ahead," Hoffin stated. "Here is where I have got to stop."

Seeing the disbelieving look on Byron's face, Hoffin added, "I got myself into a plot of trouble last year, chasing some hard cases over the border. In that part of Chihuahua, the Mexicans have gotten themselves a touchy governor. He would be on the telephone to Washington in a flash to report and possibly jail me with a grin."

"So you can't go in?" Byron asked.

"Nope."

"Well, I sure as hell can."

"Yep. Reckon you can, all right." Hoffin gave Byron a wink and a grin.

Byron immediately wheeled his horse and began to ride south, leaving Ross and the other man alone. He heard Hoffin call out after him, "I would watch you down there if I were you. They don't take too kindly to gringos."

Byron never turned; he just kept riding straight south, towards Mexico.

18

BYRON ARRIVED AT THE RIO GRANDE

Fifteen minutes later, Byron arrived at the Rio Grande. The river appeared shallow but comprehensive, and he quickly crossed it, now finding himself in Mexico. As darkness enveloped the landscape, there were no visible signs of the men he pursued. Their tracks remained elusive in the obscurity. The moon had not yet risen, and the overcast sky offered no starlight. Byron thought about dismounting and using matches to locate the fugitives' trail. However, he realised that doing so might reveal his position to the men lurking in the darkness, waiting to see if the posse followed them. Byron made a calculated decision: he would head deeper into Mexico, following the logical path the fugitives likely took. Moving cautiously, he remained alert for any signs or sounds that might betray an ambush.

His journey led him slightly west of the south. Sometime after midnight, the moon finally emerged, casting enough light through the thinned cloud cover for Byron to discern the details of the surrounding countryside. The terrain was primarily sandy and brushy, with soft ground that could reveal recent tracks. Yet, despite his vigilance, he found no trace of the men he pursued. Uncertain if he rode away from them or towards them, Byron resolved to rest and resume the hunt honestly the following day.

Byron's night had been harsh—a cold camp on the soft, sandy soil. He lay there, fully clothed, with his horse's reins looped around his wrist. His rifle rested across his body, and his right hand was near his pistol's butt. As dawn approached, he stirred, feeling slightly stiff. He retrieved dried meat from his saddlebags, its hardness offset by its nourishing properties. Mounting his horse, he chewed the tasteless sustenance as he rode. His purpose was clear, and Byron retraced his steps to where he had lost Ross and the other man in the darkness.

About half a mile from the Rio Grande, he intercepted their trail. Their direction was unmistakable: south-east. Had he continued riding in his initial path, he would have only increased the distance between himself and Ross. Determined, Byron pressed on, the chase intensifying with each mile. The trail stretched ahead, imprinted with wind-blown sand, a testament to riders who had passed hours earlier. Byron pressed onward, and a small pueblo materialised in the distance as the sun hung midway in the sky. A cluster of adobe shacks and sagging corrals formed the heart of the settlement. The tracks led unswervingly into the town.

Byron, ever watchful, manoeuvred through the arroyos carved by flash floods, skirting the outskirts. There, he glimpsed fresh tracks heading out the other side. Ross and his companion had ridden straight through, undeterred. Determined, Byron resolved to enter the town. He had exhausted his jerky rations and was hopeful that the town could provide him with supplies and water replenishment.

The pueblo revealed itself as a miserable, poverty-stricken enclave. Its inhabitants were scarce; a pair of men dozed against adobe walls, their bedrolls shielding their faces from the harsh sun. Halfway down the single, dusty thoroughfare stood a cantina, a beacon of sorts. Byron tethered his horse outside and approached the makeshift entrance: a ragged cloth covering a rectangular opening in the thick adobe wall.

Byron, ever the cautious wanderer, slipped into the dimly lit room, avoiding the harsh light that streamed through the entrance. The bartender stood behind the counter, his gaze disinterested. The only other occupant was an old man, draped in tattered garments and half-reclining on the bar. A spilled glass of mescal lay near his right hand. Byron's parched throat prompted him to inquire, "You got any beer? Cerveza?"

The bartender's nod signalled affirmation, and he produced a dusty bottle. Byron counted out a handful of silver coins, parting with fifteen cents—a steep price, but thirst outweighed thrift. The beer, despite its weathered exterior, surprised Byron with its flavour. The Mexicans, he recalled, brewed damn good beer. Standing at the bar, he drained the first bottle with long swallows. Then, having acquired another, he retreated to a small table near the room's rear. He settled there, amidst heavy wooden furniture and a looming sideboard, with the door providing a discreet vantage point.

Just in case hunger gnawed at him, Byron inquired about food. The bartender summoned a woman from a back room. She waddled in, her ample figure contrasting sharply with the bartender's gaunt appearance. Their conversation hinted at a marital connection. The bartender relayed Byron's request, and after a quarter-hour, the woman returned bearing a plate of tamales, fried beans, and tortillas. She placed it before Byron. As she turned away, the bartender brushed past her, heading back to her domain.

"Treinta centavos," he informed Byron.

Byron handed over the thirty cents and then delved into the meal. It was damn good—the tamales brimming with meat, the cornmeal perfectly cooked. The food's fiery heat suited Byron's palate, a taste he'd acquired from years spent in the West. The second beer helped douse some of the flames. Despite the lack of meaningful conversation, this place offered sustenance aplenty. Byron naturally intended to inquire about the two other gringos who had recently passed through town once he finished his meal. As he wiped up the last of the beans with a piece of tortilla, he mentally rehearsed his rusty Spanish.

But just then, the curtain covering the doorway shifted, and three men entered. The daylight streaming in momentarily blinded Byron, but as they advanced, he discerned that all three were Mexicans. Gunmen, unmistakably. No vaqueros or cowpunchers here. Their attire, though ragged, exuded a certain flair: embroidered vests, snug charro pants, and broad-brimmed sombreros. Their boots jingled with hefty spurs, rowels dragging along the floor. They were heavily armed; each man carried two pistols and at least one knife. Bandits, no doubt. They swaggered into the bar, behaving as if they owned the place because, in a way, they did. In this remote corner of the world, their arsenal could secure whatever they desired until someone tougher and meaner crossed their path.

Byron didn't escape their notice, but with a single contemptuous glance, they chose to disregard him. Turning towards the bar, they collectively ordered tequila, a luxury in a town as impoverished as this. Their boisterous conversation prominently featured the word "gringo". Meanwhile, the old drunk slumped over the bar and roused himself. After scrutinising his new drinking companions, he wisely rose and staggered out the door. The bartender, too, retreated towards the cantina's back rooms, wary of the brewing tension.

Byron finished the last of his beans, pushing the plate away. As he did, one of the Mexicans pivoted to face him—the largest of the trio. This man possessed rugged handsomeness, thick black hair, and a drooping moustache. Adjusting his sombrero, he offered a smile that leaned more towards a sneer.

In Spanish, he uttered words that Byron deliberately ignored. Switching to English, he confronted Byron:

"Ey, gringo. What brings you down here, in our country? Lost?"

Byron remained seated, meeting the man's gaze without speaking. This man considered himself the group's leader, adorned in the most extravagant attire. His once-elegant vest bore food stains, tarnishing its appearance. Twin pearl-handled Colt .45s rested in a double belt rig, crisscrossing his waist. Byron couldn't help but ponder the weight of all that iron nestled in the billet loops; indeed, it was a burden for any man.

Undeterred, the man advanced a few steps, his grin unwavering. Byron remained seated, subtly adjusting his right leg to facilitate quicker access to his .44 revolver if needed. The Mexican observed the movement, and his derisive smile waned. When he met Byron's gaze, he found no trace of fear, only a calm, lethal focus. Byron harboured little concern for the burly Mexican or his companions. For men like them, opportunistic bandits accustomed to preying on the vulnerable, like the beleaguered bartender, three against one likely didn't appear favourable. Already, the big man's expression hinted at a desire to extricate himself gracefully from the predicament his bravado had thrust him into.

Perhaps he could have found an exit strategy if the door curtains hadn't parted again, ushering in two additional figures. As the light momentarily blinded Byron, he soon discerned their identities: Boulder Ross and another gringo. The stakes had just escalated. Byron's caution kept him still, and he adjusted his posture to maintain his readiness. Now, a more formidable adversary stood before him. Why was Ross here? Hadn't he ridden out of town? Byron berated himself for not verifying the tracks—too eager for beer and food to ensure the hoof prints matched both ways. It could have been anyone leaving the far side.

"Well, well, well," Ross drawled, smiling at Byron. "Speak of the devil, and damn if he doesn't show up."

Byron recognised the second insincere smile within minutes. He withheld his own. "Afternoon, Ross," he replied coolly.

"Yeah, your last," Ross retorted, devoid of bitterness and almost cheerful.

"That's what Dean Phillips tried to tell me," Byron shot back. "Only it didn't quite turn out the way he planned."

Ross lifted his eyebrows. "Have you failed to fall for Dean?"

Ross shook his head and replied, "Well, he was more talk than action."

"Van de Velt?" Byron inquired. "Is he with you?"

"Van de Velt?" Ross repeated. "A big man like him, accustomed to the comforts of life, doesn't take kindly to riding outlaw trails when he can't just mosey back home to his little wife and sweet kids after a hard day's work robbing banks," he said.

"Where did he head?" Byron pressed.

Ross shrugged. "I think it's San Francisco. If he had any brains, he'd leave this godforsaken country like I just did. But I reckon he hates making it permanent—leaving his wife and sweet kids for good and ever. Why are you asking? You think you'll live long enough to ride after him?"

"All in good time, Ross," Byron replied. "You're next on my list... Before Van de Velt, after Dean. I owe you one. More than one for what you did. You, Phillips, and Van de Velt."

Ross chuckled. "To the girl? Yeah? I guess you feel that way. The boss figured doing something like that would get under your skin. He's a real thinker. Well, it was a lot of fun, all right? But... speaking about owing people," Ross continued, his voice lowering into a deadly snarl, "you sack of shit. You're playing your martial tricks on me. I'm going to take you apart really slowly. Perhaps a bullet through the knee, followed by a final strike with my hands."

The odds were stacked against Byron. Ross's companion, a menacing stranger, stood guard by the door. If both of them closed in on him, he would find himself caught in the crossfire. And then there were the Mexicans, with the odds now more in their favour, five against one. They seemed familiar with Ross and well aware of the quality of the help backing them up. The pearl-handled Colt revolver likely played a significant role in motivating the prominent man to take action. Alongside this, he carried a heavy burden of machismo—a need to constantly prove his manhood. This internal pressure drove him to confront challenges repeatedly, even until his final moments. Unfortunately, his demise arrived sooner than anticipated.

Stepping forward, he faced his adversary once more. With a hint of menace, he addressed the other man: "Now, gringo pig, perhaps you're ready to talk?"

"No," Byron retorted, leaning back. The Mexican man had positioned himself squarely in front of Byron, effectively blocking his view of Boulder Ross and the man near the door.

"Get out of the way, Jean!" Ross's voice boomed, but it was futile. Jean's hand had already rested on his gun's butt. Yet, his surprise was evident when he realised Byron's .44 revolver was already in his grasp. His shock deepened as the .44 roared, delivering a heavy slug to

Jean's chest, propelling him backwards towards Ross and obstructing Ross's line of sight to Byron.

Byron quickly rose from his chair and rolled to the side. Neither he nor Ross could fire at each other effectively. Instead, Byron turned his attention to the bandits at the bar. With three precise shots, he felled both of them, their screams echoing through the room. Meanwhile, Jean continued to collapse, desperately clawing at Ross as he fell, and further ensnaring his adversary. Byron swiftly sought refuge behind the sturdy furniture near his table. Ross's henchman fired a bullet just inches from his head, grazing the wood. In retaliation, Byron's shot scraped the man's shoulder, prompting him to seek cover.

Without hesitation, Byron reached the rear door, a strategic position he had chosen in advance. As he stepped outside, Boulder Ross's bullet splintered the door frame behind him. Ross urged his companion to follow Byron. However, Byron warned against using that door, fearing for his safety. He retorted, "No way. I don't want to risk getting shot in the rear."

Ross, frustrated, accused Byron of being out of ammunition. Certainly! Let me provide a more precise and detailed paraphrase of the passage: Byron's situation was straightforward: like most sensible individuals who didn't want to accidentally shoot themselves, he carried only five rounds in his trusty Remington revolver. The space under the hammer remained conspicuously empty. During the intense altercation at the bar, he expended every one of those precious rounds. Now, as he sprinted towards the safety of an adobe building approximately twenty yards away, he focused on reloading efficiently.

Rather than laboriously reloading all chambers, Byron adopted a methodical approach. He deliberately extracted one spent cartridge, swiftly inserted a live round, and then deftly rotated the cylinder five clicks to the left. This manoeuvre ensured that a freshly loaded chamber was now poised for action. The stakes were high, and Byron's survival depended on his speed and precision. The adrenaline-fuelled urgency drove him forward, leaving no room for hesitation.

Ross's henchman burst through the door, relieved that no bullets had found their mark yet. Like Byron, he squinted against the harsh outdoor light but quickly regained his senses. He caught sight of Byron sidestepping around the adobe building. Determined to outflank Byron, he fired rapidly, each shot gouging sizable holes in the adobe wall. His goal was to reach the building's corner before Byron could secure better cover. However, fate intervened. Byron stood his ground, calmly turning and cocking his revolver. From a mere three feet away, he delivered a fatal shot to the gunman's chest. The man collapsed, his life fading away in gurgles. Byron wasted no time. He circled to the building's rear, deftly reloading his pistol.

Meanwhile, Ross had announced his intention to approach from the other side. True to his word, Ross sprinted towards Byron, pistol in hand, his body low to the ground. Ross was no fool; he spotted Byron just as Byron spotted him. In a split second, Ross dove behind the cover of a horse-watering trough, narrowly evading Byron's retaliatory fire. Byron grudgingly acknowledged Ross's marksmanship as the bullets forced him to retreat once more, seeking refuge behind the adobe structure. The tension escalated into a deadly game of cat and mouse. Both Byron and Ross knew that revealing too much would invite certain death. They weaved through the town's narrow streets, sniping at each other, each attempting to set up an ambush that would catch the other off guard.

Remarkably, no one dared interrupt their lethal dance. Perhaps this forsaken little pueblito had grown accustomed to such wild gunfights. But the standoff couldn't last indefinitely. It reached its climax when Byron and Ross unexpectedly cornered each other. Simultaneously, they were startled, their surprise causing them to recklessly discharge their remaining ammunition. The pivotal moment unfolded outside a modest tienda that sold farm and ranch tools. With empty chambers, both men heard the ominous click of their pistol hammers falling on spent rounds.

Byron regained his wits first. He sprinted across the roughly twenty yards separating him from Ross, reaching for the large bowie knife he always carried at the rear of his belt. To his dismay, it was gone—lost during the chaotic brawl. Yet retreat was not an option. To turn away now would expose his back to Ross, who struggled to reload. So, fuelled by adrenaline and determination, Byron charged forward, colliding with Ross so forcefully that the other man dropped his pistol.

Byron found himself in a life-or-death struggle with Ross, who was notorious for his immense strength and penchant for beating men to death with his bare hands. In their current face-off, Ross aimed to deliver a decisive blow to Byron's throat and strike him in the groin. His formidable physicality demanded that Byron keep him engaged, preventing any advantage. Byron instinctively pressed his head into Ross's chest, forcing him backwards against the weakened door of the small tienda. The door, its hinges worn by years of use, gave way, and both men stumbled into the shop's interior.

Ross broke free first, his hand diving into a pile of discarded handles, scattering them in all directions. His fingers closed around one of the stiff wooden shafts, ready for whatever desperate move came next. He advanced towards Byron, the wooden shaft held high, a look of murderous triumph illuminating his eyes. But Byron deftly evaded the blow Ross aimed at his head— a strike that would have fractured his skull if it had landed.

Ross had scattered the rest throughout the room in his haste to secure one of the pick handles. Byron stumbled away from his adversary, heading towards the door. His hand closed around one of the handles, the cool hickory providing a reassuring grip. Emerging onto the street, Byron regained his balance and turned to face the tienda.

Ross burst through the remains of the door, his pick handle poised over his head, ready to strike. However, Ross halted abruptly when he saw Byron waiting for him, another pick handle raised high. Prudence prevailed; neither man rushed in blindly. A pick handle wielded by a strong adversary demanded careful consideration. Byron mirrored Ross's caution. The two men circled each other warily, their wooden shafts held defensively, each seeking an opportunity to gain the upper hand. In that fateful moment, it was as though an unspoken agreement had been forged between them—a silent pact to settle this violent confrontation once and for all.

The pick handles swung with brutal force, each man driven by a singular purpose: to emerge victorious. Sunlight glinted off the polished wood as they clashed. Both combatants skilfully deflected most blows, preventing an early resolution. Yet neither escaped unscathed; each scored painful hits. Panting, bloodied, and fuelled by adrenaline, they persisted, locked in a grim dance of equals. Then, like a lightning bolt, Byron's memory resurfaced—the words Ross had uttered in the dim confines of the cantina. Ross's vile comments about Abigail, the atrocities committed by him and his cohorts, and the twisted pleasure he had derived from it all.

A maddening rage engulfed Byron, a crimson mist obliterating pain and fear. Driven solely by the desire for retribution, he charged forward, heedless of danger, intent on one thing: ending Ross's life. In a decisive showdown, Byron and Ross engaged in a brutal fight, with their pick handles swinging with lethal intent. Sunlight glinted off the polished wood as they clashed, each man skilfully deflecting blows. Bloodied and panting, they continued their evenly matched struggle. Suddenly, Byron's memory resurfaced of the vile comments Ross had made about Abigail and the atrocities committed by him and his cohorts. A red mist of fury enveloped Byron, and he charged forward, heedless of pain or danger, driven solely by the desire for retribution.

Byron shattered Ross's left arm, then smashed his right hand, causing him to nearly drop his weapon. Ross suffered broken ribs on his left side, grimacing from the pain. What followed was an execution, a relentless swing of Byron's pick handle, extinguishing Boulder Ross's life. Only as the mist cleared did Byron fully comprehend the devastation he had wrought. Ross stumbled, disarmed, and was battered. His face bore the marks of a brutal beating, both arms were broken, and his kidneys were pulverised. One knee gave way, leaving him a shadow of his former self. Somehow, he managed to get on his feet.

Most of all, this may be adage, or maybe only reflex bloodlust on Ross's part, that cleared the rage from

Byron's mind, and now he only wanted to end it. He raised his pick handle high, aiming at Ross's head. Ross didn't have the strength to duck or bring up his shattered arms. The broad, hard tip of the pick handle cracked against his forehead with the sound of a million drops on concrete, and now Ross finally fell. His forehead split down the centre, his eyes unfocused, and he stared in different directions. He fell heavily. His arms and legs quivered for another few seconds, and then he lay still.

Byron shoved the bloody tip of the pick handle against the ground, leaning on it as he fought to regain his breath. He prodded Boulder Ross once with his tool. There was no movement. The man was dead. Another one for Abigail. More vengeance. An ugly vengeance. As he wearily turned and headed for his horse, Byron wondered what Abigail would have thought and what she would have said if she had been looking down at what was left of Boulder Ross. He'd never know. There was no way he could ask her.

19

DANIEL VAN DE VELT

After his altercation with Boulder Ross, Byron made a beeline for San Francisco. The swiftness of his journey was astonishing. The most challenging leg had been the arduous ride back up to southern Texas, where he eventually found train tracks. From there, he boarded a northbound train, retracing his steps through Denver and Cheyenne and heading directly west to California. The transcontinental railroad, operational for over a decade, had revolutionised travel in the West. Previously, crossing the formidable Sierras into California had been a challenging endeavour. Now, a mere three or four days on a train brought one to the Golden State remarkably easily. However, this newfound convenience came with a downside: even inexperienced travellers from the East could effortlessly reach the Western frontier. The vast, open spaces that Byron cherished would vanish as the land filled up.

Initially, Byron hesitated about venturing to San Francisco. Boulder Ross's mere mention that Daniel Van de Velt might be in the city had been casual, but it transformed into near certainty when Byron received word from the Chicago office. They had indeed spotted a man matching Van de Velt's description in San Francisco. Byron put his persuasive skills to the test by convincing the United States marshals to delay any action until he could personally assess the situation. Despite the purple bruises from his fight with Boulder Ross, Byron was alive, unlike Ross. Now, it was Van de Velt's turn to be the boss himself.

Byron was en route to meet one of the marshal's operatives stationed in San Francisco. This very person had initially spotted Van de Velt. The rendezvous point was atop one of those notorious hills. Byron had no intention of walking; he had heard the clanging bell of another marvel of the age, the cable car. Breaking into a run, he boarded the side platform and let the cable car carry him up the hill. The ease of travel in this changing world was both remarkable and unsettling. Soon, even tenderfoots from the East would find their way to the

West, and the vast, open spaces Byron cherished would vanish.

The last time he had been in San Francisco, Doc had to beg him to practically take the cable car. Byron had been reluctant to part with the quarter fare. But now, as he rode the cable car again, he appreciated his decision not just because of the steep incline but also because of the breathtaking view as the vehicle ascended the hill. The vast blue ocean lay beneath him, extending beyond his sight. Closer in, the docks were a dense forest of masts and funnels from numerous ships. Across the bay, the hills displayed their customary autumn hue. And all around him, the city hummed with life. This was no makeshift Western town with false-front buildings and dingy saloons; it was a genuine city, the only one Byron had ever truly liked.

After disembarking from the cable car at the hill's summit, Byron made a short walk to the modest restaurant where he was to meet the marshal's operative. As he entered, he spotted the man seated at a rear table, a nondescript figure hunched over a schooner of beer. Byron took a seat across from him.

"Howdy, Robert," Byron greeted him, nodding.

Robert grinned, wiping beer saliva from his mouth. "Howdy yourself. It's good to see you're still alive and kicking after your escapades out in that damn wilderness."

Byron returned the smile. Robert, a town worker, lacked the patience for the rugged life on the trail. Yet he'd pursued wanted men through territories rougher than an old whore's tongue, cursing the hardships all the way, but getting the job done.

"Are you hungry?" Robert asked.

Byron's nod prompted a steak recommendation. "They're good here, and a steak is something a man like you can appreciate."

Byron let the jibe slide. Doc used to tease him similarly. As they prepared the steaks, he remained silent. However, when Robert continued extolling the virtues of San Francisco's food and his fondness for the city, Byron finally interjected.

"Where can I find my man?"

A pained expression crossed Robert's typically good-natured face. "Well, now, that might not be so easy."

"What the hell?" Byron growled, half rising from his chair. "You haven't let him—"

"Take it easy, Byron," Robert pleaded.

Byron suddenly understood why Robert had been so eager to discuss other matters. He was expecting bad news about Van de Velt.

"Come on, spit it out," he snarled.

"Well, now we think we know where he is," Robert said hastily. "Well, we might know pretty well anyway."

"How close?"

"He may be a bit up the coast."

"How many miles?"

"About three hundred miles away."

"Oh, OK."

Once he saw that Byron was not about to murder him, Robert loosened up enough to tell the rest of the story. About a month ago, he first noticed Van de Velt, drawn to a man whose face resonated with him, though he couldn't pinpoint the reason. Robert commented that he certainly didn't resemble a bandit. He lived at the Palace Hotel, which doesn't precisely cater to the likes of Byron. The Palace was one of the city's newest and probably most expensive hotels. It is big, with more than 800 rooms and an enormous courtyard.

"He was almost emaciated. His eyes were dark voids; they bled not with light, but with loss. The absence of his beard was evident—a stark change from the man Byron had known. Byron's .44 pressed against Van de Velt's gut, and the trembling banker was caught off guard as he stepped out of his room. The once-debonair man had deteriorated. Days-old stubble covered his face, and his hands shook, though not from fear. Van de Velt strained to regain composure.

"So now it's over," he rasped.

"Yep."

"Well..."

"Well, what?"

Byron's hesitation lingered. Why not pull the trigger? Hadn't he come here to kill Van de Velt, just as he had ended Phillips and Ross? All three had wronged Abigail, but this situation felt different. Phillips was sitting on the bed, waiting for a bullet.

"Uh-uh," Byron finally declared. "I'm taking you in."

"You'll hang."

Real panic etched Van de Velt's face. "No! You can't do that. My family, my wife, and my children... They'd hear about it. They would be aware that their father faced a common criminal's execution by hanging. They might even watch. People do terrible things to children. You... have to shoot me!"

His plea erupted into a scream. Byron recoiled, then regained his resolve. "Walking into your room and blowing a hole in you won't look good," Van de Velt said.

"Uh-uh. I'll let you in, and you'll face the gallows."

"No! You can't! My God, you must want to kill me. Remember what I did to the girl."

Van de Velt's obscene description of Abigail's final hours pushed Byron to the brink. The urge to pull the trigger surged within him, yet he resisted. Instead, he resolved to bring Van de Velt to justice, letting the law decide his fate. The outlaw needed to hang. However, Van de Velt sensed Byron's determination, reading it in his face. Suddenly, with astonishing speed, the man lunged. Byron, accustomed to desperate pleas for death, now faced a frenzied assailant. He tried to sidestep, unwilling to fire, but Van de Velt's right hand swung towards his head. At that moment, something Van de Velt had picked up connected, and stars exploded within Byron's skull. He plummeted, his consciousness slipping away. The room spun, and darkness claimed him.

Byron fought to remain conscious, knowing that Van de Velt would kill him if he blacked out. The banker tugged at Byron's .44, but he clung to it with determination. A curse from Van de Velt, and suddenly, the man was no longer before him. Sinking to his knees, Byron struggled to see clearly. A zone of blackness, tinged with red, clouded his vision. But gradually, clarity returned, and he forced himself upright. His head throbbed, and he gingerly touched the source of pain. Blood, but not too much. What had Van de Velt struck him with?

Now, the room came into focus. The door stood closed, and Van de Velt had vanished. Byron approached the door, attempting to open it. The knob turned quickly, yet the door remained stubbornly shut. Van de Velt had wedged something beneath it. Outside, shouts echoed from the street, followed by hooves thundering. Byron kicked at the door, splintering it until it abruptly swung open. A man with an angry expression confronted him in the hallway, one hand gripping the chair he'd pulled away from beneath the doorknob.

"What the hell is going on in there?" he demanded. His face paled slightly upon spotting the gun in Byron's hand.

"I'm after a man," Byron snapped. "The one who was staying in this room."

The man hesitated, still eyeing the Remington. "You missed him, then. He just stole a horse from out in front and rode off."

Byron dashed outside. The small group of men stood together, their fists shaking in anger as they gazed northward. His mount waited on the far side of the plaza. Vaulting into the saddle, Byron caught their attention.

"He's headed up towards the Trinidad Road!" one of them shouted after him.

Kicking his horse into a fast canter, Byron followed the man's pointing finger. There was no sign of Van de Velt yet, but the dense forests offered few escape routes. If Van de Velt remained on horseback, his choices were limited. Byron maintained his pace, wanting his mount to stay upright during the chase. During his raids, he recalled how Van de Velt had emphasised the importance of caring for their horses. Now, that concern seemed absent.

Byron encountered men walking along the roadside, about five miles up the trail. He halted to question them.

"Yep," one of the men said. Just a few minutes ago."

An undeterred Byron pressed on. As Van de Velt rode in panic, he might pull away temporarily. But when his horse tired, it would be Byron's chance to close the gap.

Half an hour later, Byron arrived at the tiny hamlet of Shawlands. Perched above a deeply curved bay, the town consisted of only a few houses and a solitary lighthouse. Here, the land opened up slightly; perhaps the ocean winds discouraged dense tree growth. Byron's gaze swept down the coast, where a thick smoke cloud hung over Eureka. Millions of acres of forest stretched inland, and the air felt clearer and the sun more intense.

Questioning the locals, Byron learned that Van de Velt had ridden through just minutes ahead of him. When he explained that he was pursuing a horse thief, the townspeople readily cooperated.

"You'll get him, mister," one man assured him. "The trails lead to dead ends further up. He was riding a really worn-out animal. I doubt it'll last more than a few additional miles."

True to their prediction, the horse didn't hold up. About a mile along the trail, Byron discovered Van de Velt's stolen mount. The animal knelt, breathing heavily, its fate uncertain. As the man in Shawlands had warned, the trail essentially dead-ended there, narrowing significantly. Van de Velt's boot tracks vanished up a narrow track to the left. There was barely enough space for a horse. Byron urged his mount onto the path. While he hadn't noticed a gun on Van de Velt, that didn't mean the outlaw was unarmed. Riding cautiously, Byron scanned for ambushes. Though prickly enough to hinder movement off the trail, the sparse cover wouldn't effectively conceal a man.

The trail ended a couple of hundred yards farther along, and Byron emerged onto a broad meadow bordered by brush and small conifers. The sea lay about a hundred yards straight ahead. He spotted Van de Velt, still running but staggering from exhaustion. Van de Velt looked back, glimpsing Byron as he attempted to accelerate. Yet there was nowhere to escape. In this open expanse, Byron could quickly close the gap.

Byron nudged his horse into a trot. Van de Velt swerved to the side. Byron kicked his mount faster, aiming to cut him off. The meadow was on a small plateau above the ocean. At its seaward edge, the high bluffs were too steep to descend. Van de Velt had no escape. Byron herded him towards the cliffs, riding from side to side. Soon, Van de Velt stood pinned against the precipice, a drop of at least a hundred feet behind him. Exhausted, Van de Velt had no choice but to halt. He faced Byron, his expression wild and panting.

"It's all over, Van de Velt," Byron shouted.

Van de Velt glanced back at the sheer drop behind him, then turned to face Byron. His demeanour had shifted; he was calmer now.

"Yes," he said, his voice barely audible over the crashing surf below. "It's all over. All over now."

As he peered down the cliff once more, Byron understood his intent.

"No!" he shouted, urging his horse closer.

Van de Velt took another step backwards. "Tell my wife," he pleaded. "Tell my children... No. Don't tell them anything. Let them believe I disappeared."

Byron's rope slipped free. Perhaps that was how his wife and children had known him—not as the efficient bank robber, the ruthless outlaw, but simply as a man, a husband, a father. Byron's horse refused to approach the cliff edge. Dismounting swiftly, he raced towards the precipice, and then pulled back. Wind and rain had eroded the edge, leaving him half-suspended in space. He crouched down, studying the shoreline below—a tumult of rocks and waves where land met sea.

And there, amid the bleak expanse, he spotted Van de Velt, a small patch of colour with blood spreading around his broken body. The water quickly washed away the evidence, and a colossal wave surged forward, obliterating everything in a storm of spray and white foam. When the wave receded, Van de Velt had vanished.

Byron lingered at the cliff's edge, his eyes fixed on the churning water. He thought he glimpsed Van de Velt's body bobbing about fifty yards offshore, but uncertainty clouded his perception. Finally, he turned away from the abyss. Standing next to his horse, he grappled with his emotions. Cheated? No. Just a peculiar emptiness. The men who had taken Abigail's life were no longer with her. With each death, his ties to her unravelled, one by one. Vengeance, he realised, was a flavourless dish.

Swinging back into the saddle, Byron glanced again towards the cliff, then set off slowly along the trail. None of it had brought Abigail back. He was alone again, as he had been long before. Perhaps solitude was his destiny—a purpose he had been shaped for, and the ache that lingered within.

THE END.... OR IS IT?

BLURBS

Once a herald of justice, U.S. Marshal Byron earned his moniker "The Huntsman" through the relentless pursuit of lawbreakers across the nation. His life, a testament to the power of the law, changes irrevocably with a personal tragedy. Now, driven by a searing quest for vengeance, Byron's mission transcends the badge. In a gripping narrative of retribution, follow "The Huntsman" as he navigates a dangerous path where the line between justice and vengeance blurs.

ABOUT THE AUTHOR

At 73, after the loss of his beloved wife Annie, the author embarked on a journey of fulfilment and remembrance by penning the book they had long envisioned together. Encouraged by her enduring support and reminded by his sister Janet of a lifelong aspiration, he has woven a narrative that is as much a tribute to his late wife's memory as it is a realisation of his literary dreams.

Printed in Great Britain
by Amazon